Romeo's Juliet
Book IV: Family Affair

By Devin J.

Hard work and tears went into this book. I dedicate this to my fanfiction friends, my crazy family and people who not only support me but those who doubt me.

xoxo,
Devin J

000. Lost

She was the last person he wanted to call but he knew as much as she despised him at times, Jan was there when it counted. She sat across from him staring at the bags under his eyes and the worry all over his face. She was shocked when he called pleading for help with his fiancé. It had been six months since Mia had attempted to kill Anjel and even though she survived, losing their son took a toll on her.

"We don't talk, she doesn't go anywhere, she barely eats. She won't do shit ma. I love her an' there's nothin' I can do to help. Li tried but I don't think anything can fix this."

"Losing a child and almost dying isn't fixable."

Jerome sunk into his chair and released a heavy sigh. "What do I do?"

"I wish I knew! I just came here because you sounded bad. You've never been one to give up. Just don't give up on her. Let her grieve."

"I have! Bellz and Li are afraid to say the wrong things so they been distant." Ro was so frustrated and Jan could tell by the shade of red that covered his face.

"Just let her know that you're here you love her an' don't treat her like you'll break her because she's already broken."

"I wish Mia was alive so I could kill her again."

Jan turned her cheek not caring her son's lack of filter.

"I just want things to be like they were."

"Things are never gonna be how they were. This changes things this changes her. Just be there for her. Call me if you need me. I gotta go to work. I love you."

Rome sat still for a minute pondering how to save his relationship long after his mother got up and showed herself to the door. "Fuck," he groaned as the sight of her lifeless body flooded his mind. Mia may not have killed his girlfriend but she did something worse by killing her spirit.

...

Quietly she sat on the bedroom floor staring at Aliyah's face flashing upon her phone screen as she called for the second time in a row. She kept telling her she was fine but she insisted on talking every day. "Hello," finally she picked up not wanting to talk but knowing Aliyah wanted to at least hear her voice.

"I'm fine. I'm still here...just like yesterday and tomorrow and the next day.."

Li sat quietly for a few seconds hesitant to speak. She knew her sister was lying but she didn't know how to help. "I just want to talk." Li finally spoke feeling the weight of the world on her shoulders. "I don't know what to say or how to help you an' it scares me because I know you. I know everything about you. I can't keep pretending."

Gi felt her eyes watering as she heard her sister's voice break holding back tears.

"You're not okay. An' I've-we don't know how to make you okay."

Gi sniffled wishing her pain was physical, at least she could tolerate it but the ache in her heart couldn't be bandaged or mended. The one thing she wanted was gone and all that was left of him was an empty nursery. "Bye! Love you!" She interrupted Li's emotional downpour and pressed end.

Her hands touched her wallpaper on her phone displaying the last sonogram. Her sorrow was soon mixed with rage as he remembered begging for mercy. Quickly she stood to her feet and stomped as her feet led her across the hall to the nursery. She stood in the doorway remembering how she had their future planned out and she had failed to ensure he had one. Feeding the fresh anger that onset, she stared at the basket of baby clothing at her feet and kicked it across the room spilling the contents. She wanted to cry so bad but she had no more tears left. She was so fuckin tired of being sad she just wanted to feel something else.

"Gi..."

She froze after picking up the framed sonogram on the table next to the window. Her heart ached at the sound of his voice. She didn't have to turn around to know he was standing in the doorway.

"I need to," He started and he paused startled as she threw the frame across the room before turning around and staring at him. His hazel eyes were fixated on trying to read where she was emotionally. So far all he had gotten was sadness but today something was different and he wasn't sure if it was good or bad.

"I'm so sorry," she started. He stood confused as she walked over and wrapped her arms around his waist making it the first time she had touched him in a while. "I couldn't protect our son. I'm bein' unbearable. I had one job. I understand if the wedding is off."

Ro wrapped his arms around her waist holding her tightly pained at the fact that she blamed herself. "It's not your fault an' I would never leave you."

"I'm a mess," she argued whining pressing her cheek against his chest.

"I know. I just wanna be here for you. I want to be the reason you smile again." She closed her eyes feeling his arms loosen as he placed his hand under chin forcing her to look into his eyes. "We're gonna get through this an' we're gonna get stronger. I need to be here for you. Tell me what you need an' it's yours."

She gently bit into her bottom lip trying to find anything to numb the pain. She was cool with the anger she was harboring. She saw the ache and concern in his eyes and realized her brokenness was starting to reflect on him.

In an effort to save the both of them from a painful conversation she pressed her lips against his and passionately kissed him. He pulled her closer returning her kisses and parting her lips with his tongue. Her hands snaked around his neck.

"Gi," he started catching his breath feeling her lips attacking his neck. Internally he was questioning where this was coming from. He had seen more emotions from her in one day than he had seen from her in months.

"I need you," she whispered in his ear almost pleading for anything other than sadness.

Passionately he kissed her lips giving her what she wanted. Gently she pulled away before removing his shirt. He kissed her again breathlessly and slowly pushing her out of the room and across the hall.

"Mhmm," she whined feeling his two fingers massaging her lips as he hoovered over her on the bed. "Ro!" she gasped moving her hips to the rhythm of her fingers massaging her.

"I love you," he whispered pausing to remove his sweats. He stepped out of his boxers and quickly picked up where he left off.

She closed her eyes feeling his lips caressing her neck and her body felt as if it was melting as she felt him take his time inside of her. "Ahh! Ro! Faster!" She barely got words in between his kisses.

"Faster?" He questioned and she nodded opening her eyes staring at him.

"Yes! Like that!" She gasped feeling him go faster and deeper and she blocked everything else out and focused on him for the moment wanting this so bad. This was her blissful distraction. "Ahh! Uhh! Fuck!" She moaned as he leaned completely pressed against her body hands grasping hers above her head. "Jerome," she let out a breathless scream arching her back as much as she could as she unraveled under him. A few strokes later her body was elated to feel his juices drinking down her legs. Silence filled the room as he positioned himself besides her knowing she would be the first to break it.

"Your year is almost up." He smiled remembering the ultimatum she gave him soon after he proposed.

"I got you. I just need you to take care of you." She nodded resting her head on his chest bored with the idea of talking about her state of mind.

She was enjoying her bliss and just wanted to sleep for the first time in a long time. She knew it was short lived but she needed to savor it. He was her forever.

"We need to get rid of the nursery." Turning over and facing him she quietly spoke. "I can't though." He nodded understanding what she was saying.

"I'll take care of it. Anything else?"

Gi huffed pondering her needs hoping the huge breath she exhaled could push every inkling of sadness into the air. Her grief and guilt drowned her and she was tired of swimming in it. "Maybe if I try to work again maybe it'll keep my mind occupied and I'll feel better."

"Maybe. Maybe you should stop blaming yourself. Nothing that happened was your fault. I don't blame you. I love you and know you did all you could to save our kid."

Gi's eyes watered as she thought about her baby. Ro's words were nice but nothing comforted her. She was responsible for his life and she couldn't even bring him into this world. She would give anything just to hear him cry. "I didn't save him!"

"You barely saved you babe and if I had to pick, I'd always pick you. You did everything right."

"I just wish everything could go back to how it was. I was planning our future. I pictured the perfect house, the wedding an' my career and our son." a faint smile spread across her face as she replayed her fantasy.

"We'll get there on day. I promise."

"That doesn't help. The pain isn't physical. Mia broke me. She did worse than kill me. She took the one thing I would've given my life for. You probably think that's a terrible thing to say but that's how I feel."

Ro nodded as he stared at her lying on her side facing him. He wished there was something he could do to make all her pain go away but it wasn't physical. "You can't help how you feel. Do you wanna?"

Gi shook her head not letting the *b* word escape his lips. "You can't just replace one kid with another. It's not the same. I don't think I could look at another kid let alone think about carrying another one. Maybe one day."

"This ain't your fault." He would repeat it until she believed it. "Truth is I was excited to start our family but I was also excited to know you weren't dead. I couldn't live with myself if something happened to you."

"I love you too. I'm thankful you were there. I just wish it was all a nightmare but it was real an' walkin' past an empty nursery reminds me every day."

"It's cool, I'll get rid of it. Anything you want within reason," she nodded knowing she could be unreasonable. "I got you. Plan our wedding or honeymoon shit! Whatever you gotta do to get your mind right, do it! I'm here an' I'm not going anywhere.

Always and forever...

001. The Anjel Show

"Are you, even listening to me?" Aliyah glanced from Austin to a spaced out Rome as the three of them sat watching TV in Rome's unusually untouched living room.

"Let me find out he over there daydreaming 'bout his wedding." Aus chuckled taking a sip of his beer. "Aight! So when's the big day? What's the details 'cause this been under way forever." Finally he questioned attempting to be serious.

Ro sighed sitting back sinking into the black suede couch. "Whenever Bellz and Gi come up with a date. I told Gi she can handle all that just lemme know when she get the bill. She hired Bellz to plan it an'…"

Both Aus and Li couldn't hold their laughter long enough for him to finish his thought.

"What?" He asked super confused to why they were amused.

"Bellz is doing no such thing!" Aliyah was sure Bellz would've run that past her first.

"Gi said," Ro paused knowing there was only one way to settle their argument. Pulling out his phone he tapped Bellz name and put it on speaker.

"Yooo," she was quick to answer.

"Where you at? You busy?"

"No, and home for once. What's good?"

Ro glanced at Aus and Li before asking the question at hand. "Are you planning my wedding?"

Bellz chuckled surprised by the question. "Well, I could but you would have to pay me and I would need the okay from Gi. When's the big day?"

"I don't know. I'll let you know later." Rome didn't even say goodbye before hanging up the phone and shaking his head.

"Wooow! Anjel lied about this whole wedding situation. Shocking," Li teased Ro knowing he was pissed. "She's been on a high okay. If you're not a camera or a catwalk she ain't interested. She's hiring an assistant and I've seen her on TV and in the magazines more than in person now a days."

"Speakin' of," Aus interrupted Aliyah's banter staring at Gi's face on the television screen.

After the game stay tuned to your ten o'clock news. Local celeb Gigi Monroe is having quite the year. She's opening Gigi Boutique, starting a modeling agency, and she's making moves to ensure that Angel Entertainment is a powerhouse. She just signed a 45,000 dollar deal with B Magazine. We got the details on the deal and who else is involved."

"Well at least y'all won't go broke with this wedding shit." Aus was the first to break the silence.

Ro and Li knew she was making moves but never that kind of money.

"She's about to blow."

. . .

"Please tell me that's not permanent." Mickey pleaded staring at a fire engine red head Anjel.

Gi smiled from ear to ear before plopping down in her office chair across from Mickey ready to go over this B Magazine contract. "It's semi it'll take a while to come out but I love it."

Mickey nodded not wanting to hear that answer but just going with it. "This deal is contingent on you getting back to pre-baby weight. Exclusively attending B Magazines events for the year and B Magazine gets any exclusive interviews from you."

"I've been trying to lose weight." Gi pouted watching Mickey tap her pencil as the two of them sat in the Gigi Boutique office going over her new contract. "I want to eat everything in sight an' I don't. I try working out and nothing is working. I'm eating less and gaining weight."

"We have to try harder." Mickey spoke so politely almost to the point where it annoyed Anjel.

"I look like a fuckin' whale." Gi folded her arms across her chest upset with herself for not being able to control her weight.

"No you like you had a baby." Mickey corrected.

"That's just it! I didn't, but I got you. I'll try harder. What's on the agenda for the week?"

"Focus on you an' getting this place finished. We're spending money when we need to be making it. Also, the samples that came in please okay them."

Gi huffed making a mental note of the things she could control. A halfway finished Gigi Boutique was on course to be one of the hottest apparel shops in the Brooke and after lingerie she was fazing in jeans. "Can you oversee all of this madness? I'm goin' home to look at the samples and what not. Maybe I'll also question my diet and life choices." Gi semi-joked standing to her feet.

"I got you maybe while we're looking over these applications you haven't stared at. You can find an assistant so I can manage you."

"I got it! I got it! Love you Mick!"

...

"Whaaat? You do exist!"

Gi smiled seated on the living room floor surrounded by a sea of samples and a stack of employment applications. "Hi to you too."

"One of us is way busier than the other. How's wedding planning with Bellz going?"

Staring at him standing in the doorway she opened her mouth and quickly closed it at loss for words.

"It was easy to lie the first time but you can't do it again? When were you goin' tell me?"

Gi scratched at her messy red hair quickly searching for the right words to why she lied. "I look like a whale! I can't fit in my own clothes. I was gonna ask her when things died down. I need to lose weight. My endorsement deal is contingent on that."

"I didn't propose 'cause you were smaller than you are now."

She smiled amused by how carefully he choose his words. "It's now my turn to ask you for time." Getting up she quietly spoke walking over to him and wrapping her arms around him.

"How much?" It was impossible to stay mad at her for long.

"Two, three months? I wanna go back to my old weight."

"You know what burns calories right?" He smirked brushing his lips against her neck. She stood there feeling like she could melt as he gently pushed her body against the wall. She had been working so much she'd almost forgotten how it felt be touched.

"Mhmm," she moaned feeling his lips attack her neck and his hands slide up her black skater skirt. "Ahh," she leaned back feeling his fingers ignore the thin fabric of her *Angel* lace panties and gently massaging her lips. "Roo," she whined getting closer as he went faster.

"Gi," he started leaning in whispering her ear feeling her lips getting wetter and wetter.

"Jerome," she groaned opening her eyes in awe that he completely stopped.

"I'm still kind of pissed at you." He stepped back and folded his arms across his chest staring her down.

"Fuck me," she groaned not knowing where this twisted conversation would lead. "Can we do this after? I'm an asshole. I know this. I love you."

"Gi," he groaned watching her unbuckle his belt. "Gi," finally he swatted her away grabbing her wrists and she gasped staring in his hazel eyes.

"What do you want?"

Finally, she said the magic words and he smiled. "If you had to pick one day would you pick me or this job that has you always gone?"

"You," she answered quickly. "I need you honestly. This job ain't goin' keep me warm at night. I do need time."

"I need honesty. I need your time." Ro insisted trying to set some ground rules.

"I need you to fuck me!" Gi smiled speaking firmly one track minded.

Ro nodded amused to how they got back to square one. "I need you to be here maybe cook sometime, ask me how my day was."

"Done. Done. How was your day? Steak or shrimp?"

"Yes, you are an asshole." He smiled letting her wrists go. "I see more of you on the TV than in person."

"Clear your Friday. I'm all yours after 2pm."

"And we don't have steak or shrimp because no one is ever here to go shopping." Ro sighed staring at her hoping she was listening to what he was trying to get across.

"We'll go out to eat my treat."

Ro stood silent for a second too long because Gi huffed like a child and went to walk away but was stopped when he grabbed her hand and pulled her towards him. "You goin' buy me dinner fo' real?" He whispered standing behind her.

"Yes," she spoke slightly annoyed and turned on. They were twisted but it was fun. "Ro," she went to speak and paused feeling Rome's hand palming her behind.

"Where you want."

He smiled pressing her body between him and the wall. Slowly he pulled her lace panties to her ankles and she smiled glad to have gotten her way and to have avoided an argument.

"Oh shit! Ro," she groaned surprised by the lack of warning.

"You said you was ready," he teased.

She placed her hand on the wall arching her back as he entered her from behind and placing her free hand over his. "Gentle," she insisted knowing this was his favorite position. "Ah! Ah!" She barely got her moans out feeling him pumping faster and faster. She moved her hand on the wall for leverage and he gripped her waist feeling her meet him halfway. "Oh fuck!" She breathlessly moaned feeling him spank her behind. He pulled her closer feeling her walls suffocating him.

"Take it don't run," he smiled loving the view of her ass up face down running her fingers through her own hair. He felt accomplished as she let out a load moan before the two of them were dripping in each other's juices. They stood there for a minute basking in the high.

"Where you wanna eat?" She broke the silence turning around and staring at him fixated on her.

"Let's go to Mae's. I want a burger. We should really fuck more often."

"Noted," she agreed. "Why are you staring at me like that?" Finally, she questioned placing her red tresses in a messy bun.

"You! Wondering what kind of sorcery you have. I want you to be my wife no matter how small you are."

"Give me like two months to drop this weight."

He rubbed his chin noticing it was almost like the baby weight never left. "When was the last time you had a cycle?" He chose each word carefully and she still scoffed.

"Boy I don't know. Don't curse me with your hopes and dreams. I'm busy."

"Just a thought! That can only explain gaining weight on a fuckin' diet."

Gi rolled her eyes smiling at him. "You bask in all that by your lonesome. I'm gonna shower."

. . .

"You've hooked this place up. I see a salary is doing you well."

Bellz playfully rolled her eyes letting Aliyah in her one bedroom apartment in Woodcrest.

"Your apartment looks way better than my house. You live closer to my sister than I do."

"Yup! Apparently, I'm planning her wedding. September 28th. The day they got engaged. Something about losing weight. Want a slice of pizza?"

"Of course! What have you been up to Miss Manager?"

"Life! I met a new chic who doesn't have baggage and she's hot as fuck."

"Is she," Li raised her brow curious to what such a woman existed.

"Nope! She's never been a stripper. She came in as a part of a bachelorette party. Honey was fuckin' hot. She looked all uncomfortable in the strip club. It was cute."

"What's her name?" Li leaned over the breakfast bar excited for Bellz.

"Kori. She's a journalist fresh out of college."

"You got pics? She sounds make believe as hell. Lemme find out you be praying on college girls." Liyah teased her in between giggles.

As soon as Bellz grabbed her phone a knock on the door interrupted them. "Who is it?" Still on cloud nine she sang peeking out the peephole.

"Who," Li mouthed and Bellz shrugged cracking the door.

"Who is it?" Bellz questioned again staring at the young woman finally staring at her face. "No way."

"Izzy? Isabella!"

Bellz huffed before opening it all the way, letting the girl in and quickly scrunching up her face in disgust at Li.

"I can go if," Li started not really wanting to leave.

"Stay please," Bellz never took her eyes off the woman who stood 5'5", had the same butterscotch brown complexion and almond shaped brown eyes. "Ivy meet Li. Li meet Ivy. My little sister."

"Whoa! Wow!" Li smiled knowing she was in for a treat because Bellz family practically disowned her after discovering she was a lesbian.

"You're Gigi Monroe?" Ivy questioned starstruck for a second.

"Nope! I'm her twin and Bellz' best friend."

"Oh, I was gonna say damn girl weight loss looks good on you but I guess she's the chunky twin."

"What, do you want? How did you find me?" Bellz folded her arms across her chest ignoring Ivy's rudeness. She hadn't seen or spoken to her family since they gave her the boot five years ago, but Ivy was still just as ridiculous.

"It was really hard but it's important." Ivy's playful tone changed as a cloud hung over her mood. "Dad is," she inhaled a breath of air before continuing. "He's dying and I want... and mom she wants..."

"Absolutely not! Why does he deserve peace? Since in his words I'm goin' to hell..."

"If it makes you feel any better I'm goin' to be sitting right next to you. He hates me too. I told him I was bisexual and he told me there was no such thing."

"Sooo? You gave him a heart attack?" Bellz raised her brow at her baby sister confused.

"No! I refused to leave and mom refused to allow him to run all his children away. That doesn't stop him from condemning me to hell for bein' a heathen." Ivy paraphrased her father's words amused. "He did kick me out of the congregation." She paused heartbroken that even though her father didn't like her, he loved her and she dreaded using past tense to describe her father's actions. "He has cancer. He didn't ask but he and mom would appreciate."

"I was goin' through a tough time in my life. He literally left me out in the cold."

"The man is dying Izzy! Let him apologize." An agitated Ivy rolled her eyes disappointed in Bellz' response. "I have a test to study for. It's very nice seeing you're okay. I'm gonna leave my number and you call when," Ivy emphasized *when* "You decide to come around."

"You don't have to," Bellz insisted watching her scribble her number on a piece of mail on the breakfast bar.

"Nice meeting you Li. You look stunning." Ivy smiled at her sister and then winked at Aliyah before heading out the door.

"Your sister though," Li smirked trying to lighten the mood and pouring the both of them a drink. She could tell Bellz was going to need something stronger than wine so she poured them both a rum and coke. "She fine as hell."

"Oh really? Let's trade." Bellz giggled at the thought of Liyah and Ivy. "She's a lot. Didn't expect her to be bi though." Bellz took a seat on the sofa and sighed as Li put a glass in front of her.

"So you gon' see your father or nah?"

"Thanks for easing into it." Bellz sarcastically spoke staring at Li sitting across from her. "I don't know."

"Take it from someone whose father was scum of the Earth. You only get one set of parents."

"If the tables were turned. Would you want Gi to go see your dad?"

Li froze thinking about all the hurtful shit her father ever did to Gi. "That's different." Li sat back sipping at her drink. "He put Gi through hell. He broke her. I had to put her back together again and again. She won't even go to his grave. She threatened to kill herself leading up to the day she fuckin' snapped."

"Would you go see your mother?"

"Noo," Li paused realizing where the animosity was coming from. "Just think about it. If I had the opportunity maybe. I would've saved his life to avoid the shit with Gi that came after I don't want you wondering what if. Let me see this girl of yours." Li quickly changed the subject and Bellz smiled picking up her phone and pulling up a photo of Kori in an all-white bikini. She looked like a model fresh off somebody's runway. "She's fine as hell are you sure she's?"

"Oh she is! She's definitely not as innocent as she looks. It goes down. The sex is fuckin' amazing."

"Okay. Invite her to the Gigi Boutique Party. I gotta meet her."

"That you do. She thinks your sister is a fuckin' rock star."

"Find me somebody 'round here who doesn't." Li rolled her eyes amused how Gi could always be the topic of discussion. "For a $45,000 endorsement deal she better be a fuckin' rock star. I see her more on TV than in person."

. . .

"I come bearing presents." Gi smiled putting down the employee applications hoping Mickey had something that would brighten her day and her smile slightly fell at the sight of her holding the gorgeous dress that she knew she couldn't fit. "It was designed just for you. I need you to try it on while I go track this lost shipment. Please find an assistant so I can be your manager."

"I got you. I don't know what I'd do without you Mick."

"Lose your mind that's what." Mickey smiled placing the dress on a hook beside the door before heading out to make some calls.

Anje sat there staring at the gold ensemble hanging up almost as if it was mocking her. She put down her pen, stood to her feet and shimmied out of her black short sleeved skater dress. She grabbed her designer gold dress and placed one foot in after another. The gold mermaid short sleeved dress was something out of her dreams. It had a scoop neck that would show off all her cleavage and the velvet crush material would invite everyone to touch her. There was just one problem. "Fuckin fuck," she groaned feeling the zipper snag on the material as she attempted to force it all the way up. "Noooo," she attempted to shimmy out of it beyond frustrated that she couldn't get the dress completely on or off. "Mickey! Mickeyy!" She screamed wanting to cry. "Help me!" She felt like the longer she stood in the thing the tighter it became.

"Are you kidding? I'll call you back." Mickey walked in and immediate wrapped up her conversation. She pressed end, put the phone in her pocket and huffed trying to unzip the zipper on Gi's dress. "Suck it in!"

"I'm trying!" Gi cried. "Cut the designer a check cut it off!"

"Okay! Okay!" Mickey tried consoling her scanning the office for scissors. She grabbed them off Gi's desk and immediately went for the zipper area. "I need to find you a trainer and an assistant and you should go see a doctor because you're gaining weight. We need you to lose it."

"I'm trying." Gi whined stepping out of the gold ensemble. "I don't wanna go to the party."

"Not an option. You're the face of B Magazine. What have you been eating?"

Gi huffed putting her black skater dress back on and staring at Mickey in defeat. "I don't know. Take the rest of the day off while I get this figured out. I promise tomorrow we'll regroup and form some kind of plan. I'm leaving early too. Love you much." She felt a sense of relief as she watched Mickey walk out of the room leaving her alone with her thoughts.

"Shit, shit," she groaned staring at the picture of her in one of her first designs. Gigi Boutique was going to be an empire and she literally couldn't fit into it. "Did you forget?" Anje was interrupted from her trip down memory lane by the sound of the hot pink bells on the front door ringing. She just assumed it was a busy Mickey forgetting something and was a little thrown off looking at Gotti standing in her doorway. "Hey you," she put on a smile not really wanting to socialize but not wanting to seem like an asshole.

"What's up? I been tryna holla at you an' nobody returns my calls so I figured I'd swing through."

"That's news to me." Gi couldn't recall ever getting his message and then she put two and two together. "Mickey manages my business calls. She works for me but Rome might have a little influence." She sighed jotting down her personal cell number. "We're coworkers sort of. Here's my cell. Don't share it or I'll change my number." She semi-joked handing him her card.

"I'm tryna get you on a hook an'…"

Gi laughed genuinely amused not allowing him to finish his statement. "I'm a model not a singer. I'm not even a great singer."

He smiled expecting her reaction. "Your fans like me, my fans worship the ground you walk on."

Gi playfully rolled her eyes before sitting back in her chair hearing out his proposition.

"You ain't gotta be great. Just good. Think 'bout how many singers are great now a days. The studio will handle the rest."

"Okay, that's something to think about. You wanna perform at this fashion show?"

"That would be dope. I actually came to ask 'bout my friend Winter. She wanna model in it."

Gi nodded jotting down the girl's name. It was obvious she wasn't walking in the show. She could use someone to take her place. "She any good? Can you send me her info? I'm kind of tired. I'm actually taking the rest of the day off."

"Aight! I hear you. Think about that track. I want you on my next album."

Gi nodded amused by his enthusiasm. "I gotta run it past the not so silent partner but I got you." Gi grabbed her purse and headed out behind him and as soon as she got to the front she sighed exhausted by the sight of the stranger standing at the counter. "See you Gotti." She waved goodbye to him before bringing her attention to the young woman staring at her with a huge smile.

"Stella! Stella Scott," she introduced herself confidently handing Anje her resume. "I really really want to work here. I live down the street and I've been working up courage to ask. I'll do anything." Stella had passion and Gi saw it in her dark brown eyes. Stella was oozing with enthusiasm.

Glancing down at the cream-colored paper Gi yawned staring at the young lady's credentials: *MBU Graduate with a BA in Writing, Six years of Admin Experience…* "What kind of job do you want? You're overqualified for retail. I wouldn't…"

"I know but I studied writing. I don't care if it's cleaning up the place or whatever." Stella was not giving up.

"How about my assistant?" Gi thought out loud.

"What assistant?" Stella scrunched up her face confused.

"I need an assistant. Someone to answer calls, maybe get me food, remind me of meetings, hire people, fire people, you name it. It has odd hours because you would be on the team and…"

"I'm in. When I start?"

Gi smiled staring her down admiring her ambition. "10 AM. Here's my cell. Call me when you're outside. I'm leaving which means you're going home to rest. You goin' need it child. Welcome to The A Team."

002. Ring the Alarm

On the outside, she was smiling but inside she felt her stomach sinking lower and lower into the pit of her stomach as she walked beside her younger sister. The walk down the dreary hospital corridor seemed like an eternity. Most people would be excited to see their parents after years but Bellz was not most people and excitement was the last thing she was feeling.

You don't owe that man anything. She remembered Aliyah's words. Stopping at room 216 Bellz stood in the hall for a minute and put on her best smile as Li instructed. *You've done well for yourself. You didn't need them then and you don't need them now. Do this for you.*

"Oh my word!" Nina gasped as her youngest child walked in with Bellz behind her. She hadn't taken Ivy serious when she said she was going to find her sister but no one took anything Ivy said at face value. Ivy enjoyed proving them wrong.

"Where's dad?" Ivy smiled nonchalantly standing in front of her mother.

"He went for some test," Nina answered never taking her eyes off her first born and trying to hold back tears.

"I'm gonna grab a muffin from the café. You said you wish you could be with all your children. I made that happen. You're welcome."

Bellz shook her head as Ivy winked at her before walking out of the hospital room leaving her alone with her mother. For a moment Bellz stood by the window staring at Nina who at 50 was aging gracefully. She stood there in a navy blue maxi dress and a pair of white sneakers. Her salt and pepper shoulder length hair was pulled back into a ponytail. She had always been beautiful on the outside.

"I'm sorry," Nina finally broke the silence walking over to her to look her he in her eyes. "It wasn't the Christian thing to do. I regret it every day."

"You could've stopped him. You could've stepped in." Bellz nodded not knowing what an apology was supposed to do for her. "You two always made me feel so low, so small and I wasn't gonna…" Bellz continued to stumble over her words. "My best friend whose parents are actually dead an' shittier than mine told me I'd regret it if I didn't show up. I tried to think of something that would make me feel better an' I got nothing because before Ivy came knocking, I was happy."

Nina nodded trying to understand her daughter's point of view. "Understand how…"

"I did nothing wrong!"

"Your decisions." Nina interrupted not seeing Bellz' side. "Affected this entire family. I didn't want you to leave but your sister." Nina's eyes welled with tears and Bellz scowled realizing they blamed her for Ivy's sexuality.

"Newsflash being a lesbian wasn't a choice, it's not fuckin' contagious, it's always been who I am and you guys were too damn blind to see it."

Nina shook her head in denial. "Why," she cried. "Why are you like this? We wanted the world for you."

"You thought I'd grow out of being myself and be who you wanted me to be? That's delusional." Bellz smiled ignoring her mother's tears. It was obvious she hadn't changed. "I manage a nightclub, have a very nice apartment, a best friend and a girlfriend who thinks the world of me. I could bring you the world… the fuckin' solar system and you'd still be unhappy with me because I'm a lesbian." Bellz folded her arms across her chest disgusted with her mother.

Nina sighed mirroring her daughter's body language trying to find the words to make things right but she knew there were none. They would never see eye to eye. "This was a terrible idea. Please leave."

Bellz chuckled nodding her head in agreement. "That's something we can agree on."

"Please stay away from Ivy. There's still hope for her. We can fix her."

Bellz rolled her eyes and looked back at her on her way out. "Good luck with that. She found me." Bellz quickly walked the halls red in the face and the first thing she did when she stepped foot outside was text Li.

That was not the happy reunion I hoped for. I did everything right. Ladies night, my house…bring wine.

…

"Stella can you please call these people for interviews an' then call Gotti about the model he wanted to walk in the opening."

"Is everything okay?" Stella watched as Gi sat at her desk. On the outside, she looked polished but her behavior was a bit frazzled.

"Yes, that's it! Also, if Mickey comes just send her back she's my manager." As soon as Stella walked out of her office Gi locked the door and returned to her chair. She sighed removing the sonogram from under the *no* portion of applications.

That's a heartbeat Miss. Monroe. You were right to come in. You're very pregnant. I give you one or two months before he or she arrives. I can't tell the sex. Congratulations...

She placed her knees to her chest hugging herself overwhelmed with the news. Tears filled her eyes petrified at the thought of losing another baby. She let out a huge breath trying to calm her tears before picking up her phone and taking a picture of it captioning it *help me* before pressing send. It took all of thirty seconds before a selfie of her and Aliyah flashed upon the screen.

"What the actual fuck? Why does it have today's date on it?" Li sounded frustrated hoping she wasn't implying that she was with child. Anjel could barely handle the first there was no way she could handle another child and Aliyah knew that.

"Because it's from today." Gi spoke with no emotion in her voice.

"How far are you?" Li was super hesitant.

"A little over seven, eight months."

"How? When? You just lost a kid like...ohh! That was quick. Your nervous breakdown on the nursery floor." Li put the pieces together. "Does Rome know?" Li changed directions.

"...No."

"Oh-kay! Where are you?" Li already knew the answer.

"Hiding, in my office."

"I'll be there in ten. Stay put."

...

"You gotta tell him ASAP! The good news is you're not fat."

Gi blankly stared at her twin seated across from her not amused by her attempt to lighten the mood. "There's nothing wrong with being fat. As long as I was happy. I haven't. I can't love a kid right now. I haven't grieved."

Li frowned up her face super concerned with her words not knowing what to say. "As usual you were dealt a shitty hand Gi. You're out of options here. You're havin' a baby. I kind of feel like this isn't an us conversation. It's a you and Rome conversation. Also, if I can love someone other than the two of us you can love that baby you're carrying."

Gi shook her head objecting. "You don't understand. I'm afraid to get attached to it. I was sitting on the bed at the doctor's this morning and I felt like an elephant was sitting on me. I had a panic attack."

"Oh! That has to be healthy for this kid." Li spoke sarcastically staring at the red headed pregnant version of herself. "I love you but I can't offer you much beyond congrats, tell your fiancé, wear a condom an…"

"Knowing what you know now would you have made the same choice between me and the baby?"

"Absolutely! You win every time. 'Cause you're strong and you'll get over this and I need you alive."

"That's selfish." Anje argued ignoring Aliyah's smile.

"That's life. I think that's why I'm big sister and you're little sister. Please tell your fiancé before anyone else does. I love you. I got a thing."

Gi sighed staring across at her sister before even leaning in for an unenthusiastic hug.

"This will get way better. I promise. You could be Bellz who has a hell of a family drama going on." Aliyah shook her head thinking about Bellz' soap opera.

"Bye love! Tell no one of this conversation."

Li smiled. "Oh, I won't. I want no part of this mess. Call me if you need anything."

Gi huffed staring at the draft for her shelving arrangements which were supposed to be submitted this morning. "Fuck me," she groaned feeling the sonogram staring her in the face. *I can't tell you what you're having but its most definitely a baby.* She felt sick in the stomach just thinking about the life inside of her.

"Hey you," Anjel was pulled out of her thoughts by one of only three people who could walk in without knocking. "I haven't seen you all day. What you been?" Mickey paused placing her coffee cup down and staring from Gi to the sonogram. "Okay," she changed gears tilting her head reading the date at the top.

"Apparently, I've been pregnant for a while. Like I'm almost finished so uh, yeah I'm not fat, I'm with child."

"Good thing or bad thing?" Mickey placed her hand on her hip trying to read the expression on Anjel's face.

"Uh... bad thing. I'd rather throw myself into traffic than have a baby but uhhh... what does this mean for my contract?"

"I don't know I'll talk to Karen. We'll work something out."

"Rome doesn't know yet." Gi sighed slouching back in her chair thinking about what this meant to her. "He's gonna be ecstatic. I-I can't love this kid."

Mickey opened her mouth to speak but found no words. She picked up her coffee and took the empty seat across from her. "Maybe you'll change your mind."

"I don't think I will. Like if I knew way earlier I would've totally risked it all, including my relationship to not have a kid."

Oh shit! Mickey thought to herself only allowing the words "What now," to escape her mouth.

"I don't know. I don't have a choice now. Maybe I can negotiate a nanny or maybe my fiancé will kill me." Gi tried inserting humor into the conversation slightly terrified of having this conversation with Rome. "I literally had a panic attack this morning at the doctor's office."

"Maybe you should go home and try to relax and let me handle everything else."

"I got so much shit to do!" Gi groaned not wanting to burden Mickey. "I'm already behind."

"You're a mess. Me and Stella got this. Good job on hiring an assistant. I can be manager now. Me and her will find a store manager and all will be right with the world." Mickey assured her that work didn't stop just because of her absence.

"Please don't tell anyone until I tell Rome. I don't need that kind of drama in my life. Thanks."

. . .

"Oh shit! You're home an' you're cooking!" Rome walked in the kitchen with a smile on his face seeing her home earlier than him for once made his day a thousand times better.

"What's the occasion?" He questioned hugging her noticing she was making steak.

"No occasion." She spoke softly fixing his plate.

"You look comfortable as hell. How long you been home?" He stared at her trying to figure out what he was missing and admiring her standing in nothing but his black tee shirt.

"About two hours," she still avoided looking at him as she fixed his plate unaware that she was being observed.

"How was your day?"

"Work an' more work. I'm behind on everything." Finally, she briefly stared at him placing her hand on her hip.

"Before I start eating this delicious meal. Are you gonna tell me somethin' fucked up 'cause I feel like I'm bein' bribed or buttered up. Do I need a drink?"

She gently bit the center of her bottom lip as she grabbed a glass and poured him some cognac.

"I don't want it. Talk." Ro sighed staring at her place a drink in front of him.

"I love you," she whined locking eyes with him.

"I love you more when you're not theatrical. Spill it…" Ro stared at her intrigued to what she was hiding.

"About eight-ish months ago, on what was the nursery floor. We made a kid."

Rome smiled excited and confused as she toyed with her engagement ring.

"I'm still grieving an' work." She paused fumbling over her words. "I want a nanny."

"You ain't even have the kid yet an' you askin' for help. When are you due?" Rome refused to entertain the thought of an outsider raising his kid. "What are we having?"

"One, two months an' I don't know she couldn't tell. Hear me out…."

Ro sat back in his chair not interested in what she had to say but willing to listen.

"I need time and I really can't do this right now. A nanny would help me ease into this." She pleaded with him and he smiled at her in disbelief that she could find a way to make anything about her.

"I can't give you this one Gi. I ain't budging. I feel your pain. But you can't love this kid less because it's not what you wanted. No way a strangers raising my kid. Thanks for dinner this was fun. Anything else?" He finally picked up his drink and his plate and Anje stood on the verge of tears.

"I had a panic attack when she told me. I'm terrified of this kid."

Rome nodded respecting her honesty. "Uh, un-terrify yourself. We're having a baby and maybe if you weren't so bogged down with work maybe you wouldn't be so panicky."

"Jerome," she whined not moving.

"Gi you ain't saying nothing I wanna hear. When do I get a role on The Anjel Show? When you're done thinking about you, I'll be upstairs eating my steak." Ro paused putting down his glass in front of her and walking around her as if she wasn't there.

"I'm not," she huffed watching him opt for the bottle. "I can't love our kid."

"I can't love you right now. If you don't love our child I can't love you and I wanna love you so get with the fuckin' program and stop this."

Standing there in silence she cried wanting Rome to tell her what she wanted to hear. "Fuck," she groaned picking up her phone and dialing Li for it to ring over and over again.

I'm busy. I'll call you later, she finally texted leaving Gi to deal with her meltdown by her lonesome.

...

Quietly she crawled into bed beside him green with envy at the fact that he was peacefully asleep while she was too lazy to search for the remote to silence the TV. Even with the television on her thoughts were still the loudest thing in the room.

Congratulations, you're having a baby! The doctor's words haunted her. *Look at the feet and that's the head.* Tears filled her eyes as she found herself back at the doctor's staring her ongoing nightmare in the face. Every time she saw that sonogram she thought of her last kid. The one she couldn't save.

The one who depended on her for one job and she couldn't do it. *We did everything we could, we're sorry. He didn't make it.* Gi tightly closed her eyelids in hopes of stopping her quiet tears and silencing her mind. That became most of her night and it didn't make it any better that her husband to be didn't reach out but instead he snored the night away.

. . .

"You're kiddin," Gi groaned rolling over in the empty bed and grabbing her phone that wouldn't stop vibrating on the night stand. "Hello," she greeted Stell half-asleep.

"You have a meeting in like thirty at B Magazine. I need you up and on time. Mickey will meet you there." Stell ignored the agitation in Gi's voice.

"Okay," was all she said before hanging up the phone and lying there staring at the ceiling. She definitely deserved a gold star for getting out of bed but not even her brand new assistant was going to give her one.

So you got up extra early to avoid speaking? How fuckin mature of you Jerome. We're adults! Good morning to you too, Gi scowled at the screen before pressing send. She didn't have to look out the window to know his truck was gone but she did anyways and that made her blood boil and warranted a text. Not even the warm morning shower could melt all the stress away. Part of her wanted to sit in the tub in a ball bawling her eyes out but she had too much pride to break down again. She grabbed a pair of black leggings, a sky-blue tunic, a black blazer and her black sneaker wedges before heading out the door. Her golden-brown roots were starting to show which was the cherry to her disaster of a day.

. . .

"Good morning," she greeted the receptionist at B Magazine as she strolled in the office five minutes early for her appointment. On the outside, she was smiling but inside she was pissed and running on little to no sleep. It didn't help that Ro hadn't even bothered to read her text.

"Good morning. Glad you can make it." 29-year-old Karen Reynolds smiled as Mickey walked in behind Anjel ready to talk business.

"It's obvious this kid is gonna affect my life but will it affect our deal?" Gi sat across from her not up for small talk.

"No, it won't instead of the direction we were going, we'll just redirect. We do have to keep you out there and relevant even though you won't be on a runway. We want sole media access to all your projects starting with the fashion show."

"Done," Gi agreed not seeing anything unreasonable with her demand.

"Your wedding?" Karen raised an eyebrow staring up from her list of bullets to hit on during the meeting.

Gi scrunched up her face uncomfortable with the topic. "No Bueno. My husband to be doesn't want the media in our love life."

"Oh-kay," Karen crossed out that idea from the list and moved on to the next. "Baby's first photos?"

Gi sat quietly thinking how she could sell that idea to Rome without him flipping out and nothing came to mind. "I have to see…"

"Anjel," both Mickey and Karen interrupted.

"How about a maternity shoot." She countered sitting back in her chair proud she had thought of something.

"And that track Gotti wants you on, do it! You two are media gold. You don't have to be great. Some of your favorite singers are mediocre until they hit a studio. Talent doesn't matter. It's image and you got it. We're investing in your future. If you win, we win. Why just be a model and fashion designer when you could have an empire? Play your cards right and that kid will never have to work a day of their lives."

...

Gi smiled thinking about her deal and Tyler smiled walking over towards the bar with Gi behind her. "I'm just glad to host. This is exciting for me. Want a drink while we talk numbers?"

"No thanks. Just send me the bill and I'll pay you." The smile on Gi's face was priceless as she admired the gold accents of Club Karma that made the place look grand. From the gold light fixtures to the elegant molding on the windows, Club Karma was a gem in the Brooke and Gi was going to utilize it every chance she got.

"Sounds good to me," Ty sighed enjoying the peace and quiet of an empty Karma before grabbing her lunch from behind the bar and continuing the feast she started before Anjel's appearance. "It feels so good to eat with no baby in my face. Aus was mad because I came back to work but I'm no housewife."

Gi smiled trying to keep it together attempting to ignore the smell of salmon lingering in the air.

"Aye! I didn't know my fiancé was here." Rome interrupted their conversation coming from the basement with Aus by his side. "Hey Ty! Hey Anjel."

Anje nodded ignoring the fact that he called Anjel when he was mad.

"Are you sure you don't want a drink or a piece of this salmon? It's fresh." Ty pushed the container towards Anje and she quickly stood to her feet and covered her mouth intending to walk to the bathroom but settling for the trash can beside the bar.

"Don't mind her she's pregnant. Like super pregnant." Ro eased Ty's concerns reading the expression on her face. "We don't like each other right now but I'mma go check on her."

Ty stood appalled for a minute and then cracked a smile as soon as he was out of sight. "At least we're not them."

. . .

"What do you want?" She groaned standing in the mirror fixing her lipstick.

"I don't like you right now but I love you. Just wanted to make sure you're okay."

"I'm fine." She assured him staring in his eyes.

"Can I agree to disagree and just move on? We're having a kid who's a huge priority over anything either of us got going on and if we try this could work. Also can you be home by eight? We're having dinner at my mother's."

She nodded not looking for an argument for once. "Does Ty know this is a front?" She randomly blurted out before he could leave.

"No, and Aus would like to keep it that way." He shook his head confused.

"I could pay your mom to watch our kid while." She paused in defeat when he quickly walked out of the bathroom leaving her alone.

Don't be reckless, she told herself over and over trying to find a solution for the baby problem that would satisfy her and her husband to be.

"Just send me the bill. I'll be back later in the week to get everything situated and pay you. I have to go." She didn't even give Ty a chance to respond before bolting out of Karma.

. . .

"Hey you. Where's my son? You're early." Janice opened her front door and was shocked to see Gi alone and underdressed even for Anjel's standards.

"We're kind of arguing." Gi sighed walking and following Jan to the kitchen. "He's unreasonable." Gi leaned against the center island watching her stir whatever was in the pot. "We're pregnant again. I can't get over the first kid and he acts like it never happened. I traumatically lost a kid. I built my life in my head you know. He won't listen."

Jan turned around concerned hearing her voice crack.

"I'm terrified. I have this second chance and I don't want it. If I wasn't due in like a month I'd say screw it an' screw him but I can't love this kid." Gi paused staring down at the granite countertop ashamed of her admission. Every time she said it the words stung a little.

Silence blanketed the two of them and as soon as Jan opened her mouth to voice her concern the doorbell rang.

Gi closed her eyes hearing the sound of his voice in the hallway. It felt like someone was just rubbing salt in her wounds.

"I thought that was my fiancée's car. I've been calling you." Ro walked in trying to be cordial and not argue at his mother's house. "So we're still ignoring each other?" Rome rolled his eyes staring at her standing at the counter before refusing to waste energy on her feelings. "What you cook? It smell bomb in here." Ro went to the stove and smiled at the sight of spaghetti.

"I can give you two…" Jan spoke trying to cut the tension.

"We don't need a moment. We're good. We talked. I'm selfish the world is over as we know it but we love each other."

Gi said nothing before quickly storming out the kitchen in disgust.

"I'm not following after her."

"She said she can't love this kid." Jan repeated her words and Ro shook his head.

"She'll be fine she's just bein' a fuckin' drama queen."

Janice folded her arms across her chest not wanting to insert herself in their squabble but very concerned with Anjel's words.

"I'll help you fix plates. She'll come around."

It was either you or him. There was nothing else would do Miss. Monroe…

The doctor's words still haunted her. She wished she could forget that entire nightmare of a pregnancy. Staring at her reflection made her angry and standing in Jan's tiny powder room made her feel like the walls were closing in. *You can do this*, she told herself trying to force a smile.

Quietly she emerged from the bathroom and took the empty seat across from him choosing to sit next to Jan instead.

"Do we know what we're having?" Jan questioned piling spaghetti on her plate and Gi shrugged.

"A surprise for everyone."

"Works going to be hard with a newborn." Jan tried to lighten the mood afraid of silence.

"It will be hard but I'll manage. I always do. We just have to adjust." She twirled her noodles with her fork and stared directly at Rome.

"I'm excited to call you my daughter-in-law. You're definitely popular around here any mom would be proud."

Gi genuinely smiled thinking about Korrine and how she would react to how her life turned out despite all the odds. She was building an empire and neither of her parents instilled that motivation in her. "I can't wait to drop this baby weight to get back to modeling. It doesn't feel like work. That's the one thing in my life I can control." She sat quietly eating her food occasionally staring at Ro would sometimes catch her staring. This was their first big argument and it sure wouldn't be their last.

003. Family Affair

"Before we let you go I have to ask why lingerie?" Gi smiled standing backstage at Club Karma watching as models got themselves together for the show. She had promised B Magazine full access to the event in hopes of keeping her promise.

"Lingerie is playful, it's whatever you want it to be. Some wear it for confidence. Some wear it for their significant other. I wanted to create something intimate. The store looks and feels like a huge closet and less of a store. Next is Jeans by Gigi. It's all exclusive to Gigi Boutique. You can't even buy it online."

"Why?" Camilla questioned occasionally jotting down notes in her blue pocket sized notebook.

"All about exclusivity. I want my brand to be as controlled as possible. I'm building an empire after all."

"Thanks for your time. I know you have to go. I can't wait to see the show."

Gi smiled before shaking Camilla's hand and scurrying away. Everything had to be perfect. Especially since the show as in three hours.

"Anjel," Gi discreetly rolled her eyes as she stood organizing makeup stations and she didn't have to turn around to know her fiancé had arrived. "What part of *you could give birth at any moment,* don't you understand?"

"Hi," she ignored his agitation and observation the commotion around her. "Winter you look amazing." She smiled giving Winter the thumbs up impressed with her make up skills.

"Laurel tease your hair a bit more please," she gave orders spotting another model.

"Gi,"

She ignored Ro standing next to her objecting everything she did. "Ro," she finally responded not dropping her smile. "Am I in labor? No! Stop bein' a pain in the ass." She left him with those words and quickly dashed to Aus' office to escape the cameras and Ro's energy.

Sitting in Aus' office she felt at peace. For a minute her heart didn't feel like it was going to jump out of her chest. *You can do this*, she told herself ignoring the butterflies in her stomach leaning against Aus' desk. She stood there for a moment trying to pep talk her confidence up and the butterflies away but the more she sat still the more she felt her insides contracting.

"What is…" Mickey walked in and stopped mid-sentence seeing the exasperation over Anjel's face as she stood leaning over trying to catch her breath. "What's happening? Sit down." She was beyond concerned and not as a manager but as a friend.

"I can't. It's like cramps that come back over and over."

"How long have these cramps been hurting?"

Gi exhaled deeply. "15 minutes." She quietly spoke.

"Squeeze my hand every time you feel a cramp." Mickey went with her gut and grabbed Gi's hand and kept her eye on the clock. Four minutes from the first squeeze came another. "No just when you feel."

Gi nodded tightly grasping Mickey's hand as an unbearable wave of pain rolled over her.

"Not cramps…labor."

"What's up? The shows about…" Ty started walking in the office with Bellz and Li behind her. "Ohhh," she froze realizing what was going on. The look on Anjel's face said it all. "That's definitely labor. What can we do? What can we do?"

"Bellz I need you to grab her car out back. Ty keep the cameras busy while we go out the back and you," Mickey smiled excited for Stella and Ro to join the party. "Stell we're gonna stay and make sure the shows a hit. Ro your baby mama is in labor. Apparently, she's been labor for a while. Carry her out the back no cameras please and thank you."

Bellz heard nothing else after her name. She grabbed Gi's keys and headed downstairs and out back to start Gi's car. Everything moved so fast that she felt in a daze when Ivy hopped in the passenger seat and Li, Ro and Gi piled into the backseat. She had one mission and it was to get Anjel to the hospital and ignore the chaos in the backseat.

…

"No, no! Just breathe, don't," the nurse groaned as Anjel tried to sit up.

"I can'," she cried covering her face with her hands trying to hide her tears in a room full of her loved ones. "I need drugs. I need this thing out of me!" She barked orders begging for someone to end her misery. "I'm in labor hello!"

"The doctor is…" The nurse sighed in relief staring at Doctor Olivia Anderson standing in the doorway. "Right here. She'll take good care of you."

Rome stood next to her beside feeling helpless as his fiancée cried.

"I want drugs! Help me!" She cried and Ro sighed reaching for her hand as the doctor positioned herself in the stool at the end of the bed.

"Okay. Let's take a deep breath." Olivia Anderson politely suggested staring at Anjel who finally moved her hands off her tear stained face and stared down at her pleading for relief. "Deep breath Anjel." She spoke trying to calm Anjel down and take control of the situation. "You're most definitely in labor. I need for only the father and two others to stay behind. Honey," Finally she looked up at Anjel as Aliyah and Bellz cleared the room. "You can do this. In fact you're pretty far along. You're not gonna have time for drugs…. You're…"

Gi gasped feeling as if her body was breaking itself to pieces. "I'm tired," she cried.

"Just squeeze his hand and push and I'll give you drugs that will put you right to sleep after all this is over. Now push and don't forget to breathe."

Gi grasped Ro's hand for dear life and grabbed the hospital blanket with the other. Every contraction felt angrier than the last and she didn't care that she looked like a maniac and her screams were deafening. She just wanted the agonizing paint to stop.

"That's it! Keep pushing," Olivia cheered Anje on glancing up at her, the heart monitor and then back down at the progress Anjel was making. "I see a head." Olivia smiled. "Keep pushing. Give me a hard one."

"I'm I'm trying!" Gi breathlessly screamed sitting up to give it her all. Ro felt her grasp getting weak so he squeezed her hand for motivation. He could see in her eyes that she needed it. Her tears were dry, her eyes were red, and her screams breathless. His body filled with relief because ten minutes of him squeezing her and her returning the favor felt like a game of It Tag, resulted in the sound of a baby's scream.

"It's a boy!" Olivia handed the small, hazel eyed baby to the nurse to clean off and everyone's smiles dropped as the steady *bee-boop* of the heart monitor went flat and a loud buzz filled the room signaling for doctors to come.

"Everyone out. She stopped breathing. I need oxygen now!"

It all seemed surreal as Aliyah felt herself being pushed out the room and she refused to go further than the doorway watching them place an oxygen mask over her sister. She silently prayed that this was a hiccup and not the end.

...

"Anjel! Anjel! Look at me. Stop! It's okay. It's okay" Relief filled Aliyah's body as Olivia glanced at La and motioned her forward. "Your baby is fine. You stopped breathing. The oxygen mask is helping you for a little. We were worried there for a minute. The medicine you wanted earlier...." That was all Anjel heard before feeling herself doze off.

"She should be fine. It was a bit much for her. She stopped breathing. We gave her pain meds and everything should be fine. "Liv smiled as a nurse walked in the room with the baby and Rome following behind. "You have a happy healthy son."

Ro's smile brightened holding the little boy who shared his eyes and golden brown hair like both of his parents. "See. That's mom." He stood over his fiancée's bed staring down at her admiring the both of them. This was his bliss. This was the moment that he realized he couldn't marry anyone else.

…

"Look who's woke."

Anjel opened her eyes staring at Rome holding a golden-haired kid and immediately froze realizing that none of this was a dream and she had just given birth to a baby after losing one with zero time to grieve in between.

"How are you?" Aliyah questioned smiling at her sister not expecting an answer.

"Hungry and I'm tired. I don't want hospital food," she whined.

"What you want to eat? You name it. I got you." Ro figured it was the least he could do after she had just given him the cutest kid any dad could ask for.

"I will love you forever if you find me a cheeseburger with everything on it."

Ro smiled before kissing her on the forehead. "I'mma remember that." He joked before handing Aliyah his son and smiling at his soon to be wife.

"What's his name? Do you wanna hold him?" Aliyah questioned mesmerized at how he was a perfect mix of both his parents. "Earth to Anjel." Li called realizing Anje was a million miles away and was either ignoring the question or avoiding it all together.

"Antonio Christopher Jones," she quietly spoke staring down at the blankets still in awe.

"Here. Hold him while I go get me a pop." Li smiled handing her nephew to his mother and quickly making an exit for the restroom and vending machines.

You can do this, Anjel coached herself holding her son for the first time. It took all she had not to cry. "I'm gonna try very hard not to let anything happen to you Tony I promise."

. . .

"Ma'am you have to go to the waiting room! We'll come get you. You're disturbing the patients."

Aliyah stopped in the hall noticing a young woman seated on the hospital floor bawling her eyes out. It wasn't the young woman's screaming that caught her attention it was her small frame and golden brown hair that she had pulled back into a ponytail. At first glance it almost looked like her older sister Alana.

"I want to see my kid!" she screamed lifting her head up from her lap and briefly freezing at the sight of Aliyah.

"You cannot sit in the hallway." The nurse scolded the stranger.

"Li what are you doing?" Aliyah heard Bellz screaming from down the hall but stood still as she was too invested in the conversation between the nurse and this stranger.

"Hey you," Bellz finally walked over and froze looking over at the distraught woman on the floor. She had golden brown hair that was pulled back into a ponytail and brown eyes that were filled with tears. "Wow!"

"Miss Monroe," Dr. Matthews interrupted standing next to the nurse.

"Yes!" Both Asia and Aliyah answered at the same time.

"Asia do you want to speak in private?"

Asia shook her head staring at the doctor. "I want to see my daughter."

"Are you relatives?" Dr. Matthews stood very confused and desperate for any help.

"Not that I know of. I just wanted to help. I'm Aliyah Monroe." Aliyah smiled trying to ease the awkwardness.

Asia stared at Aliyah quietly examining her features. "Oh! Korrine's kid?" she spoke with no enthusiasm in her voice what so ever.

"You knew my mother?" Li questioned confused and Asia nodded.

"She was a homewrecking whore."

Li smiled. "Yeah! Korrine was a lot of things. I wasn't her number one fan either. Curious though what's your father's name?"

"Anthony Monroe. Never met him. He was murdered. I got his hair and his last name though."

"Oh shit! Your life is so much more interesting than mine. I'mma check on Anje." Bellz quickly disappeared feeling the awkward tension in the air.

"He wasn't a very nice person. If you ask me you're the lucky one. You win. Like I said I'm Aliyah. I hope everything's okay with your kid. I'll be in room 213 if you wanna chat. I gotta check on my twin. Nice meeting you I guess."

"Aww! Tonio that's a cute nickname." Li walked in to Bellz holding her nephew.

"He looks exactly like Rome. Shits scary."

Gi smiled staring at them with a smile but on the inside she was terrified.

"I came back with visitors. Jo's in town an' mom likes you more than me."

Gi smiled genuinely glad to see Ro with food in hand. She watched as everyone crowded around the baby except for Rome. He sat with her while she ate and he kept smiling at her the entire time.

"Y'all are sickening." Bellz teased watching the two of them kissing. "That's how you ended up pregnant."

Gi giggled trying to ignore Bellz. "Next is the wedding. I promise." She assured him staring in his eyes as he sat next to her ignoring everyone else.

"Aliyah," Bellz interrupted staring back at the doorway noticing a teary eyed Asia standing there in silence.

"Hi," Li quickly stood to her feet and brought her attention to the stranger. "One second," she stared at a very confused Anjel. "I'll explain later promise. You rest because we're not all coming home with you."

"I'm sorry for interrupting but you were here." Asia cried standing against the wall in the hallway. "She's dead."

"Who's dead?" Aliyah stood confused.

"My daughter. She was shot. They couldn't save her an' she was my world." Aliyah's blood ran cold as Asia hugged her bawling in her chest. She was definitely blessed in the height department. 5'6" was the luck in the Monroe family.

"What about her father?" Li questioned concerned with Asia being alone.

"He's an asshole. They shot her looking for him."

"Your mom?" Li went through possible people who deserved to be there for her and Asia stepped back and shook her head.

"She hates me."

"Shit! She looks like La if La was taller, had long hair and was even remotely a hugger."

Aliyah smiled glad Aus stepped in relieved for any interruptions. "Asia meet Austin. Austin this is I guess my sister. Anthony was busy with another family."

"Aww that's much nicer than what my mother called your family?" Asia folded her arms across her chest not excited about the another family part.

"How's Gi and my godchild?"

"They're fine go introduce yourself." He said nothing else taking that as her polite way of telling him to go away. "I had an Anthony and a Korrine but I was raised by my sister who's dead. She was four years older than me and my twin. We weren't a family an' if we knew you existed growing up I would've begged your mom to take him. We grew up in hell."

Asia opened her mouth to speak and sighed wanting to compare daddy issues but too bogged down by the present. "I've spent four years being a mom with nothing to show for it. My house is a murder scene and my mother was right. I shouldn't have gotten involved with her father."

"You can stay in my guestroom." Asia's story was pulling at Li's heart strings and she didn't know why but she felt compelled to offer. "I no longer manage the club I used to work at but I'm sure between that and Anjel's endeavors we'll find you a job and have you on your feet in no time."

. . . .

004. Old Ways

"Gi," Ro groaned staring at the clock reading 2:45 AM. "Gi!" He nudged her as the cries on the baby monitor grew louder.

"I don't wanna! You," she whined rolling over with her back towards him.

"Anjel Christine," he whined nudging her again this time harder and she huffed opening her eyes and if looks could kill he'd be dead.

"You could make a bottle, you can change a diaper. You're not... I'm exhausted."

"Yeah, I did all that three hours ago, your turn." He smiled amused with her frustration and watching her quickly get out of bed and stomp out of the room with an attitude to go tend to their crying kid who wasn't into sleeping for long periods of time.

Standing in the doorway of the nursery she stared at her son who was ensuring that no one got sleep. As soon as she walked over and picked him up silenced filled the room and she rolled her eyes. "You're fuckin kiddin!" She watched as he played in her messy hair as if he hadn't been crying two seconds ago. He wasn't even two months and he was running her household. "Okay," she yawned grabbing a diaper before turning out the nursery light and carrying him downstairs to feed him hoping he would fall asleep.

What turned into *let's rest on the living room floor while I feed you*, turned into the two of them fast asleep right next to one another and oddly enough Tone didn't make another peep that entire night.

Opening her eyes she felt exhausted but also like she won the lottery at the sight of Tone still fast asleep on the floor. It was the first time she was awake before him and she was going to savor it. Quietly she got up and quickly tip toed upstairs and grabbed the first thing that matched sure to not wake a sleeping Rome.

Feeling stir crazy she grabbed her shoes, her keys and the car seat and decided to show her face at work today, baby and all.

...

Waltzing into Gigi Boutique with a car seat in hand all eyes were glued to Anjel standing in the store oozing confidence that could conquer the world.

"Good morning," Mickey greeted her in her office shocked to see her back so early and looking well.

"Good morning? I don't look it 'cause concealer, but I'm exhausted. This kid doesn't like sleep an' I'mma go crazy sitting in the house. Working mom it is. Please give me something to do."

"You could go over the samples for the denim release and approve them." Mickey paused staring at Tone stirring around in his car seat. "While you do that I'mma make some calls an' tell Stell on her way here to grab a Pack 'n Go. Also, call this guy and set up a training schedule." Mickey scribbled his name down on a Post-It before getting up and wandering off leaving her alone with Tone who sat staring at his mother quietly before he started to whine.

"You kid," she groaned unstrapping him and placing him in her lap. Just like that he was silent. "Why are you so gross," she whined watching him eat her rose pink shirt. All she wanted to do was work and all he wanted to do was to be held. It was almost like he smelled her fear and refused to be ignored by a mom who just wanted to give the minimum amount of affection.

"Shh," she quietly bounced him on her lap before picking up the phone and dialing Glenn Fox's number.

"This is Glenn," a strong baritone voice answered on the other end almost catching her off guard.

"Hey, This is Gigi Monroe. I heard you were the best and I need a trainer like yesterday. My next fashion show is in two months and I'd really like to be in it."

"How about Monday?" Glenn took her by surprise throwing out at date.

Gi stared at the calendar on the computer registering today was not only Friday but her assistant's birthday. "Monday is fine. Email me the info. I'll see you Monday. Have a nice weekend."

Hanging up the phone she stared around her office in search of anything that would make a nice last minute birthday present but came up empty handed. *Who doesn't like money*, she thought to herself before pulling at her checkbook and writing Stella a check that read *Birthday Bonus* in the memo. She placed it in a hot pick Gigi Boutique envelope and signed Stella's name on it.

"Okay, here's the denim line samples," Mickey walked in with a box and set it on the floor. "Store sales are nice and if projections are right this will be so hot that we'll have trouble keepin' it on the shelf. Also, B Magazine wants a photo shoot with you and Antonio."

"That sounds like a not so silent partner decision an' did you know it's Stell's birthday."

Mickey smiled standing in the middle of the office. "Oh shit! I did. I forgot. She told me her and her friends are going out."

"We're the worst!" Gi giggled adding Mickey's name on the envelope. "I gave her a bonus from the both of us."

"Can I get one?" Mickey joked placing her hand on her hip.

"What we giving out? Oh my god! He's adorable." Stella walked in and immediately put the Pack 'N Go box down and gave her attention to Tony eating his mother's shirt. "Can I hold him? He's so cute."

Gi smiled admiring Stella's quirky fashion taste before handing Tony over. "You look cute," she complimented her standing in a pink polka dotted white skater skirt, a white tee and some matching hot pink high topped canvas sneakers. "Also, happy birthday!"

"Aww thanks guys," Stella's dark brown eyes lit up as she spotted the envelope from Mick and Gi. "You don't have to," Stell smiled excited to hand Tony back and pick up the envelope.

"Also, if you want the VIP experience at Karma hit Tyler up and put it on my tab."

"What?" Stella smiled from ear to hear already excited for her weekend to start.

"Oh and one more thing." Gi smiled pulling out a baby bottle from the diaper bag at her foot. "Go home, the weekends is yours. You earned it."

"Are you sure?" Stell questioned through the roof already planning her outfit for the night.

"You earned it! Have fun. I would hug you but he cries when I put him down."

"You two are awesome. Thanks guys. See you Monday."

"Just so you know for my birthday I want a vacation." Mickey semi-joked taking a seat on the hot pink sofa in the corner of the room. "You should've asked Stell to open the Pack and play. You ain't goin' get anything done with him on your hip all day."

"But all he does is cry," Gi whined.

Mickey nodded staring at the little boy remembering when her son was that tiny. "Let him know you're in charge. If he's fed, changed and nothings wrong, let him cry." Mickey smiled reading the confused expression on her face. "I was like that with my first kid. After this last one I was like nope, I can't. You and Rome will thank me. Let the munchkin cry."

"I have to put this pack and play together so I can look at these jeans." Gi groaned ignoring Tony grabbing her shirt with his tiny hands.

"Speaking of Ro. Look who's here." Mickey smiled watching Rome walk in with an older version of Anjel that had to be a Monroe as the gold hair and almond shaped brown eyes were a clear give away.

"Y'all in here talkin' 'bout me?" Ro joked with Mickey greeting her first.

"Only good things of course." Mickey teased. "I'm gonna go check on the front before leaving. Also, let me know about the photo shoot. We do have a deadline."

"Have a nice day." Gi's smile dropped as soon as she finally looked at a visibly agitated Rome. "Hey, you are Asia right? Anthony's other kid?" Gi brought her attention to Asia remembering her from the hospital. She looked more rested than the last time she'd seen her. Her golden-brown locks were pulled back in a ponytail and she stood dressed in a pair of light wash blue skinny jeans and a white scoop neck baby tee shirt.

"You're Korrine's kid. I didn't know her but…."

"Asia's looking for a job and we gotta talk Anjel." Ro interrupted knowing she had nothing nice to say about Korrine. Anje was the only one who liked the poor woman."

"Okay, you're hired. I don't really need any more sales people but you're family. It pays $11 an hour. Ask Robin up front for the paperwork. Welcome to The A Team." Anje forced a smile as she walked away.

"I don't want to argue," Anje groaned watching Ro close the door.

"You had a baby four weeks ago."

Gi nodded watching him sit on her desk. "I know 'cause ever since I had him six and a half weeks ago, I haven't had a good night's sleep and I pee a little when I cough." Gi corrected Ro staring down at their son in her arms.

"When you goin' be my wife?"

She smiled at Ro realizing this was going to be an everyday thing until she married him. "Let's do it today."

"You're bein' ridiculous."

"Am I?" She sighed thinking about his proposal and the lengths he went to. "September 28th. The day you proposed. Very small wedding. Not in a church. Li will walk me down the aisle. We'll pay Bellz $1200 to plan it."

"I'm obviously in the wrong profession. Pay me $1200 to plan it."

"I'll give you more to go away." She teased placing her sleeping son in the car seat.

"When can we have sex?"

Gi rolled her eyes staring at Tony. "Your father is delusional." She looked at Ro and shrugged. "I pushed a six-pound baby out with no drugs. Let's not plot on destroying my vagina just yet."

Ro chuckled amused with her choice of words. "Since you doin' this workin' mom thing that means you goin' be home at a reasonable time."

"Very reasonable time," she assured him standing up and walking around the desk in front of him.

"So I get my happily ever after?" He kissed her forehead with a smile.

"You'll get more than a happily ever after. You let me work an' I might leave earlier and make you steak and solve your other problem."

Ro smirked pulling her close so she was standing in between his legs.

"Oh, and B Magazine...." Gi paused and he rolled his eyes knowing she was going to ruin their moment.

"Why must you ruin this?"

"B Mag wants a photo shoot with me and…"

Ro interrupted her request with a kiss. "Absolutely not." He answered knowing the photo shoot involved Tony. "I love you but Tony's not a prop."

"Babe," she whined pouting poking out her lip.

"You're a model. Our son is not anything else?"

"I love you." Gi pouted grabbing his hand and staring in his hazel eyes pleading with him.

"I love you too but it's still a no."

"Is there a gray area?" She tried negotiating.

Ro shook his head silently admiring his future wife and her hustle staring at her standing there in her rose-colored blouse and black skirt. He wanted to fuck her on this very desk but he didn't remembering the sooner that she was done working the sooner she'd be home. "You ponder on that. I'mma go see Aus an' then home. I don't want my son in magazines."

"I got it. I got it! No magazines." She groaned walking him to the office door and he smiled happy to not only avoid an argument but tie down a wedding date.

…

"Damn you ballin'" Bellz huffed as Ivy walked in her office in the middle of her counting money completely messing up her count.

"How did you even get in?" She questioned slightly annoyed with whoever was security tonight.

"I told the bouncer you're my sister and I'd have him fired. The girls here are heavenly." Ivy smiled taking the empty seat in front of the desk.

"What do you want?" Bellz questioned placing all the money in a small canvas bag to be counted and put in the bank later.

"Dinner at your place?"

"No," Bellz politely objected with a smile.

"I will show up here every day until you say yes. I'm a college student. I can afford to do it too." Ivy threatened not taking no for an answer.

"What are you studying?" Bellz sighed genuinely interested.

"Art education." Ivy proudly spoke.

"Very promising." Bellz refused to hide her sarcasm.

"Actually, I have a job waiting for me after graduation. I'll be teaching art to middle schoolers."

Bellz smiled staring up at her finally paying attention to her realizing Ivy would bug her until she said yes. "Does this dinner end with me giving you anything?"

"Time? I realized time is precious and I love mom but I miss you. It showed lots of maturity to show up even when you didn't want to."

Bellz sat back in her chair remembering her mother's warning to stay away. But while was she to break the bond between her and her sister again? "Okay! 8pm tomorrow. Don't be late. My time is precious."

"Can I hang around?" Ivy smiled already knowing the answer.

"No, you're not old enough to be here. I'm working!"

"You're not fun anymore," Ivy pouted.

Bellz rolled her eyes okay with not being fun anymore and before she could get all the way annoyed she was interrupted by the sound of her phone vibrating and smiled at the sight of a bikini clad Kori bragging about her off day.

"Ivy, I love you please go study or go college."

...

"Now you sleep," Anje smiled staring at a fast-asleep Tony in his car seat. Giving Stella the day off and sending Mickey home did give the uninterrupted focus to work on the samples and her vision for her denim and lingerie photo shoot. Even Tony cooperated a bit while the two of them sat on her office floor drowning in denim samples. Her child was an angel when he slept but awake the kid was clingy. After taking one last glance at her desk and making sure her mess was contained to the box in the corner, she grabbed her diaper bag, her keys and set her alarm before making her way outside.

"Gigi! Gigi!" Anje squinted caught off guard by the six men and two women standing outside with cameras in their hand. "When's the wedding? What's the baby's name?" She stood frozen as they surrounded her. With her diaper bag on one shoulder and her car seat in her hand it was starting to feel like it weighed a ton and the closer the photographers got the more it felt like she was drowning in a sea of people. "Gi what's up with you and Gotti?"

"Can you," Gi started not liking their aggressiveness. She just wanted to get to her car.

"What about the sex tape with you former MBU football player?"

Gi felt like she was going to choke on her own oxygen as one of the reporters screamed louder than the others.

"What are you," she started to quietly speak but was elated as Gotti broke through their small circle and came to her rescue.

"Real classy y'all. Really?" Offended he grabbed her car seat and led her to her car and hopped in the back seat.

"Thanks, just slide that right…"

"I can do it," he proudly assured her strapping Tony in as she pulled off. "Welcome back workin' woman! You need security."

"How did they even know," she whined stopping at a red light.

"You're Gigi fuckin' Monroe! You're kind of a big deal an' your office is behind your store."

Gi huffed feeling emotionally drained from the encounter but still lingering on the last question. "Where are you goin'" She questioned his destination.

"Just drive around the block. Sheesh! He look like his father." Gotti paused staring at a sleeping Tony. "We gotta talk."

"I'm listening," she stared back at him in her rear view mirror.

"You got a sex tape?"

Gi shook her head from side to side objecting the notion. "I don't. I would remember."

"Oh! But you do," he argued. "I've seen it. Some blogger from MBU has it an' ain't released it 'cause she waitin' on the highest bidder."

"I've only been with Rome and a guy who raped me but he's very much dead. You got the video?" Gi questioned scratching at her messy ponytail.

"No! I watched at it. Thomas somethin'… a missing football player." Gotti sat back slowly putting the pieces together that Thomas was the rapist and was missing because of it. The terrified look in Anjel's eyes said it all. "I needed to bring this to you 'cause you gotta be the highest bidder or part ways with B Magazine."

"You're fuckin' kiddin' me?" Gi groaned beyond distraught. This was her first day back and far from what she wanted to be dealing with.

"I wish! She run a blog called CelebriTea TV."

Gi huffed pulling over on the side of the road typing the website in her phone. "What if I pay her and she still releases it?" Gi sat skeptically scrolling down the page.

"Mickey hates me but she know her shit. She'll get an NDA and dead this tape. This needs buried. You might wanna put her on it sooner than later an' Tuesday meet me at Studio 42. Thirty minutes is all I need."

"You got it!" Gi quickly assured him ashamed of the video knowing she couldn't have been coherent. "Thanks for lookin' out." Gi unlocked the door and gave him a faint smile as she said goodbye. She sat there for a minute replaying every moment she shared with Todd, every encounter and none of them included a camera. *For fucks sake Todd,* she quietly cursed him as she pulled off and dialed Mickey's number.

"Gi, I thought you were leaving early." Mickey greeted her on the second ring.

"I did. I'm driving home now. A while back I had a guy who was obsessed with I..." Gi paused rephrasing her thoughts in her head. "Word on the street is he made a sex tape without me knowing. Most likely I was under the influence. Gotti saw it. Paparazzi may have. CelebriTea TV is offering it to the highest bidder. Can you please..."

"Got it! Please go home and relax."

...

"All that talk and you wasn't even here." Rome smiled at Anjel comfortably seated on the sectional in nothing but a tee shirt. "I almost thought you was lyin'. You super early."

"Your dinner is in the oven, Tone is sleep and another hour from now I hope to be too."

"Motherhood looks good on you." He smiled walking over and sitting next to her.

"Remember you said that," she semi-joked knowing she was bound to screw up in the future. The only reason Tone was still in one piece was because she had a whole team who helped in the office.

"How was your day?" He questioned genuinely wanting to know.

"Better when you showed up. I'm exhausted and I…" She froze as soon as she leaned in and kissed her.

"Is it better now," he questioned kissing her neck before gently pulling her on to his lap excited to know she had nothing on under his shirt.

"Mhmm," she moaned in his ear feeling his lips massaging her neck. It had been forever since they touched and Ro was determined to change that.

"Lift up right quick," he whispered before unbuttoning his pants and sliding them off with his boxers.

"Ro," she started staring in his eyes fixated on her lips as he kissed her not wanting to break this moment. "Fuck," Gi cursed herself forgetting her thoughts as his lips attacked her body. "Oh," she buried her face in his chest feeling his fingers inside of her massaging her making her wetter craving for him to be inside of her.

"You were sayin," he smiled watching her grinding against him way too preoccupied to finish her sentence.

"Rome," she groaned feeling him stop. Staring in his eyes she tried to catch her breath but never got the chance to finish her thought because she found herself on her back as he stroked deeper and deeper inside of her.

"Shit," he grunted feeling her walls suffocating him reminding him of one of the many reasons he loved her. He felt her thighs squeeze him and he quickly and passionately kissed her knowing she was going to scream any minute and neither of them wanted to be up all night with Tony.

Breathlessly she lay there basking in the well-deserved orgasm she just had and froze feeling his juices dripping down her inner thigh. "We need…"

"Noo," he whined staring in her eye still inside of her knowing where her conversation was going.

"Well, if you don't want this to be our last time you'll buy some."

"Gi," he sighed getting up slightly annoyed that she was proposing condoms like they weren't engaged. "We're getting' married."

"I don't want any more babies," she argued.

"Ever?" He questioned with no intention of listening to her answer.

"Not now. We have a baby. Let him have only child syndrome for a bit."

"Birth control?" Ro scrunched up his face trying to negotiate. "I really like feeling me inside of you."

Gi opened her mouth to speak but found no words for his honesty.

"The sectional isn't new anymore," he joked realizing it was their first time having sex on it.

"Jerome," she raised her brow staring at him standing pants-less.

"I don't want to argue. Let's table this…"

Gi laughed at him trying to pull her on her. "I'm not having sex with you."

It was now his turn to be amused. "Really? Good luck with that," he interrupted her before kissing her sweaty forehead and going to take a shower. "I love you."

Well, he's impossible…

…

"In a minute I was gonna check your pulse. Good afternoon sleepy-head."

Gi stood in the living room doorway staring at Ro and Tony in disbelief that she had slept way past noon and the world hadn't stopped. "I can't believe you let me sleep."

Ro chuckled staring at Tony sitting in his walker bouncing up and down. "You were snoring like you needed it."

Gi shook her head from side to side objecting. "I wasn't snoring."

"Sure you weren't." He rolled his eyes sarcastically agreeing with her. "Your phone kept vibrating so I grabbed it." Ro placed it on the coffee table watching her take a seat on the sectional. "Mickey handled that tape situation. You should start conversations with that next time there's a situation. I need to know."

Gi sat stunned that him and Tony had been up all morning. "I," she started and Ro kept speaking.

"I hired security for you meaning they work for you but I pay them so only I can fire them."

Gi scoffed not feeling that idea. "What do you…"

"Only I can fire them. Their job is to keep you and my kid safe. Non-negotiable. They're not friends. They're security. Oh and I told Mickey it's a no-go for the mommy and me shoot."

Gi sat impressed with his organizational skills. She was confused to rather she should thank him or be worried about his hands on approach to being a silent partner.

"I called Bellz too and offered her the wedding job."

"Since when you been so involved in my life?" She raised her brow deciding to go with worry.

"Since I invested in you." He spoke sensing her confusion. "A Thank you would've been a better response but I'll take it."

Gi huffed realizing her silent partner wasn't going to be silent especially employing her security. "Can I pick one person to balance out the security team?"

Ro shook his head not up for negotiating. "I want you safe. I trust them you trust me, all is good in the world."

"I'm still not having sex with you." She smirked, remembering their last disagreement.

"Right," Ro sarcastically spoke knowing his fiancé.

"Carrying a baby is the best birth control."

"Right?" Ro shook his head smiling at her. "Me and Tony will go pick up women who want to sleep with me."

Gi burst into laughter at the mere thought of him with someone else. "No one else will love you like me."

"I guess you right. An' it don't help that I got this super jealous fiancé that..."

Gi smiled amused with his teasing glad to be interrupted by the doorbell as an out to his madness. Their kid wasn't even one and he was trying to impregnate her and her dreams again.

"Oh, I forgot to tell you that I set up a meeting with you and Bellz."

"Thanks for the heads up," she groaned getting up to answer the door. On the outside, she was smiling at Bellz but on the inside, she was a little annoyed at Rome's meddling. "Come on in. I'mma find some shorts, make yourself comfy in the kitchen. You'll get brunch out of it."

Bellz smiled admiring Rome's persistence. "Your fiancé really wants a wedding."

"My fiancé is crazy. I don't like him in my calendar." Gi huffed walking in the kitchen and grabbing a bowl out the cupboard and eggs out of the fridge.

"Your people work for you but I think they're afraid of him." Bellz semi-joked pulling out her small tablet out her bag. "September 28th is the big day?"

"Yup! I told him no more than twenty-five people. A romantic venue that's not a church." Gi paused thinking over any details.

"Colors?" Bellz questioned jotting down Gi's words.

"Purple," Gi confidently spoke beating a few eggs.

"Ohh! Purple accents." Bellz furrowed her brow not seeing Anjel's vision. "Purple dress is a no."

"Purple tinted?" Gi inquired trying to incorporate purple.

"Oh, okay! What style?" She ignored the purple part making note to find Gi a white dress.

Gi shrugged unsure. "Halter top, mermaid fit, no pouf or strapless. Oh! Maybe lace or beaded detail." Gi threw out ideas as they came. She never imagined herself getting married so she had no dream dress.

"Bridal party?"

"Nooo!" Gi objected not wanting to pretend she had a large enough circle of friends.

"Bachelorette party?" Bellz reworded the question with a smirk on her face.

"Bellz if you must. Like six people. No bridal shower."

"Got it!" Bellz smiled widened as she watched Gi scramble some eggs. "Gimmie six closest friends. Go!"

Gi leaned against the counter before popping two bagels in the toaster. "You, Li, Tyler, Mickey, Tori... that's all I got."

"Good enough. How do beach weddings make you feel?"

"I don't care, just no churches." Gi reiterated.

"Food? What are we feeding people?" Gi huffed already over the wedding talk. "It doesn't matter to me. As long as I marry Rome and he can stop asking me when's the wedding I don't care. You think of all the details while I work on not looking like a whale."

"Your fiancé cares a lot." Bellz explained putting down the tablet.

"I've noticed. Don't remind me. He's really excited about this wedding. The only thing that excites me less is bein' a mom."

"Save the dates?" Bellz ignored her nonchalant behavior taking it as sarcasm.

"Purple with a picture of my ring as the centerpiece. I trust your judgment."

"Dresses?" Bellz tried again realizing this was going to be like pulling teeth.

"Two months from now," Gi insisted placing two saucers down.

"Gi," Bellz groaned watching her assemble two bacon, egg and cheese breakfast bagels. "If you're tryna exhaust me, you win!"

"I just wanna marry him. I don't care about the details."

...

005. Old Skeletons

"Where's Dontae? What in the world?" Aliyah walked in her house following the trail of rose petals from the front door to the dining room and stood staring at Darius a bit skeptical to why he had made a mess and who made the elaborate dinner.

"He's at my mom's. We…me an' you had plans you're ten minutes late but sit down."

Aliyah nodded slowly sitting across from him staring at the candles and roses and the two pasta dishes. "What are you up to? It's not money because business is booming for the both of us and it's not time because I've become mother of the year. What do you…" Li paused watching Darius dig in the pocket of his khaki colored cargos and pulled out a jewelry box.

"You make my life so hard yet easy at the same time." He paused opening the box and setting it in front of her. "I want to marry you."

Aliyah smiled not knowing what to say and unsure how to feel. Staring in his dark brown eyes she froze not understanding where this was coming from. It had been five years of their on and off relationship and she liked where they were. "Why?" She groaned gently pushing the ring to the side of the table.

"Because I love you. I'm tired of being your boyfriend. I wanna know if we're going somewhere. I …"

"I don't, know." Li shook her head from side to side. "I didn't see this coming."

"I don't know is not an answer. It's yes or no Aliyah."

"I love you." She assured him staring down at the ring. "Marriage is big. I don't…"

"Fuck it!" Darius grew irritated with every word she spoke. "You're impossible. You're broken and despite that I fuckin' love you."

"Darius," Aliyah screamed upset that he was angry. She sighed watching him grab the jewelry box and storm at the house, leaving her alone at a table for two. "Fuck me," she groaned pouring herself some pinot and drinking in one gulp before blowing out the candles and following behind him knowing he was already gone. "What have you done?" She quietly questioned her actions as she pulled out the driveway heading to the one person right now who could make her feel like less of an asshole.

...

"Did I interrupt?"

Bellz smiled staring at Aliyah standing at her front door with a bottle of wine in hand and a look like she had the weight of the world on her shoulders. "No," she spoke staring at Kori as she walked in the room and at the sight of Aliyah she immediately grew annoyed. "I always got time for you. Me and Kori were just finishing a movie. What's up?" Bellz ushered Aliyah in and closed the door behind her.

"Darius proposed!" Li blurted out and Bellz eyes almost popped out of their sockets.

"And?" Bellz questioned opening the wine and pouring three glasses hoping that would make Kori chill out about Li crashing their date night.

"I said why? Are you sure? And I pissed him off. The ring is fuckin' gorgeous."

Bellz raised her brow walking over and handing Kori her glass before rejoining Li in the kitchen to discuss her crisis. "Why didn't you say yes?" Kori sat confused.

"Why did you say no?" Bellz stood confused trying to read her best friend.

Aliyah folded her arms across her chest and sighed leaning against the kitchen counter. "I love him. He's amazing. It's just, it was unexpected. I don't understand why he would want to marry me. I never saw it coming."

"You guys have been together for a while though. If you love each other why not marry each other?"

"I don't want him to just be doing this because he thinks he has to." Aliyah pondered through all the what ifs and Bellz chuckled.

"He wouldn't be with you if he didn't want to. He's crazy about you even though you drive him crazy."

"What if he deserves better? What if he finds it?"

Bellz scowled at her best friend finally putting together what was happening and she almost choked on her wine seeing this insecure version of Aliyah. "First of all, I don't think he'll find better because look at you. Where do you go after you? That's like Rome trying to find something better than Anjel. You're just nervous that you'll screw this up and you probably will but no marriage is perfect."

"What am I supposed to do? He ran off angry."

"Try going home and calling and apologizing," Kori interrupted walking in with an empty wine glass tired of being on the sideline. "That's probably a good start." Kori refilled her drink and smiled standing next to Bellz.

"I could but…" Aliyah sighed bringing her attention to Bellz.

"You could and you should. Y'all been good. You just got cold feet. If he won't marry you he's crazy." Bellz tried boosting her ego smiling from ear to ear excited for her best friend. "I love you. Call me if you need me. Let me know how it goes. Give the guy a break."

Aliyah smiled placing her empty glass down and giving Bellz a tight hug. "Wish me luck. If not I'll be on your couch," she semi-joked knowing there was no way she could look at him if he refused to propose again.

"You'll be good," Bellz assured her grabbing her hand. "The two of you have been through crazier."

. . .

Hey, you've reached Darius. I'm not near my phone right now. Text me…. Or you could leave a message after the beep…

Aliyah exhaled a huge breath of air sitting back in her car and for the third time her call went straight to Darius' voicemail.

"D," she spoke quietly dreading pouring her heart out on his voicemail. It was most definitely easier than face to face. "I'm sorry. I know, I fucked up. I panicked. I don't know why but I felt like why me. I know you can do better and it scared me. I don't show it as I should but I love you and I wanna do this so," she paused pulling into the driveway. "If you wanna get married. I'm all in. I love you and apologize for being crazy." Aliyah hung up the phone, turned off the car and headed inside the house to clean up the remnants of the dinner they didn't have. After picking up the rose petals and placing dinner in the fridge she went upstairs and quickly peeled herself out of her clothes to shower. It felt like the longest shower of her life with no interruptions from either Dontae or Darius. She didn't like the quiet.

Hey, you've reached Darius…

She hung up the phone after stepping out of the shower and getting his voicemail once again. "Fuck," she groaned dropping the phone on the floor and getting into bed alone. *What if you blew it? What if he's actually done?* Aliyah sat in bed drowning in her thoughts and quickly got up realizing she wasn't going to get any sleep. Sliding into her slippers, and putting on her robe, she shuffled downstairs and grabbed the bottle of tequila out the kitchen.

"Hey…"

Aliyah jumped as Asia screamed walking into the front door. "I know D told me to go treat myself to a night out or a hotel but I…"

"It's fine," Aliyah interrupted staring at her standing in the kitchen doorway.

"Whew! I didn't feel comfy taking y'all money. What's up? Who drinks tequila straight?" Asia folded her arms across her chest questioning what she had walked in on.

"D proposed. I got super insecure. He left and won't answer my calls."

Asia placed her hand over her mouth shocked at the night's events. "Oh-kay," was the only word that came to mind as she walked over and poured herself a drink from their makeshift bar on the cabinet next to the microwave. "Why, did you say no?"

"He kind of deserves better but Bellz is right. What's better?" Li tried to convince herself that she deserved a happily ever after. "I'm probably gonna screw this up worse than my sister but I deserve this."

The room grew quiet as the two of them stood across from each other silently sipping their drinks.

"Tell me about your day. Distract me from my ridiculousness." Li insisted realizing Asia lived with her but they rarely had any moments with each other being that Dontae made it impossible for Aliyah to do anything without him.

"I've been looking into daddy's murder."

Aliyah almost choked on her tequila. "Why?" She barely got out the question feeling the burning in her throat.

"He deserves better than his half ass investigation. I'm thinking of hiring someone to look into it."

"Let's just leave those skeletons buried." Aliyah insisted staring at her as if she had truly lost her mind. "Our father was an asshole. Good riddance if you ask me."

"What he ever do to you?" Asia put down her drink and folded her arms across her chest defending her dead father's tarnished legacy.

"It's cool you have this fantasy of who you thought Anthony was but he deserved everything he got. He did nothing for me. He ruined my sister's life."

"She seems cool to me," Asia argued staring Aliyah down. "She always shoots me down at the mention of the man's name."

"I don't know," Li shrugged laying on the sarcasm thick. "Maybe because he stole her virginity and her childhood."

"Li," Asia scoffed far from amused and not understanding how she could joke about it.

"Bless the person who killed him. Face it Asia, Anthony was a sadistic sociopath who deserved worse than death. When he died me and La was all *finally!*"

"You and Gi…" Asia paused staring at her sister in awe not expecting such harshness. "Were you guys ever suspects?" Asia tapped on her glass trying to ease the tension but persistent on getting a story out of her.

"Asia," Aliyah huffed feeling her heart sink to the bottom of her chest at the sound of a car alarm and then keys jingling in the front door. "Fuck," she mumbled under her breath before finishing her tequila.

"Hey Asia what's up?" Darius greeted her not even acknowledging Aliyah's presence.

"Good. I was just heading out for some air. Your girlfriend's a jerk." Asia cut her eyes at Aliyah and Darius nodded finally looking her way.

"I know but for some reason I love her."

Asia shook her head from side to side not understanding how children could hate both of their parents. "Good luck with that."

"I'm an asshole," Aliyah was the first to break the silence after assuring Asia was gone.

"I know. I was gonna stay out all night to make you feel how I felt but I don't want people in my business an' Rome talked me out of it."

"You went to see Rome?" She stood confused to where the conversation was headed.

"Yeah and it turns out you and your twin aren't so different after all. I don't want better. I'm not gonna change my mind. I want this." He paused pulling the ring out of his pocket and placing it on the granite counter. "For some reason you don't believe you deserve the world. You got this hard exterior but I see through it. We're probably gonna fuck this up but I wouldn't want to go through it with anybody else."

Aliyah smiled staring at the beautiful engagement ring. The silver band with a diamond perched on it fit her simple taste.

"But," he interrupted her thoughts and picked up the ring. "If you say yes you gotta mean it. It's just me and you, not me, you and all those bitches you be fuckin' with."

"Wha," she placed her hand on her chest shocked he knew.

"Just 'cause I don't say nothin' don't mean I don't see it."

"Oh-kay!" She quickly agreed realizing it was either this or nothing and settling down sounded cute. "Us against the world," she assured him smiling as he slid the ring on her finger. "Just one thing." She had a demand of her own. "Let's not worry about the wedding til next year."

"Why?" He wrapped his arms around her waist.

"I don't want to overshadow my sister. I want Bellz to plan it and let's just enjoy being engaged. No rush."

"Are you stalling?"

"No," she promised. "I'll pick a date after Gi's wedding I promise. I love you and I swear I don't deserve you." Her smile brightened feeling his lips kiss hers. She was stunned this was happening not remembering the last time something great happened to her.

...Who said you couldn't have a happily ever after?...

"I didn't cook. Order pizza. Or leftovers... Tony's sleep. I'm sore. My body hurts."

Ro smiled staring at Gi sitting in bed with exhaustion written over her face.

"My trainer is trying to kill me," she joked, smiling as he sat next to her.

"You look smaller," he carefully complimented her noticing her progress. Between work, working out and minor changes in her diet she was almost back to her weight before Tony.

"What are you," she started tensing up as he placed his hand on her shoulder. "Shiiit," she smiled feeling him sit behind her positioning her in between his legs. His rough hands massaging her tense shoulders was bliss. "That feels amazing," Gi closed her eyes feeling his fingers gently dig into her shoulders.

"Ro," she opened her eyes as soon as he moved her hair from her neck and gently began massaging her neck with his lips. "What are you," she failed to form a sentence as his hand slid in between her legs and began massaging her other set of lips. Her body melted into his leaning back against his chest forgetting about her day and enjoying this as the world sat still for a bit. "Ohh," she whined quietly feeling his lips attacking her neck. "Ro, babe," breathlessly she grasped the sheet beneath them trying to keep from screaming. Seeing she was almost there he went faster making her gasp for air and lean back harder trying to keep from screaming. "I want you," she breathlessly whined. "Inside of me, now."

He stopped and kissed her forehead smiling as if she had made his day. In hindsight, she should've seen that the massage was a trap but she didn't care. It took all she had not to get up and help him undress as she watched him shed his clothing on the bedroom floor. True, her body was sore from her workout but this felt like bliss.

"Fuck...Jerome," she gasped feeling him deep inside of her and staying there. "Oh! God!" She grasped his sweaty back for dear life feeling her muscles tighten and her thighs began to shake. Staring up at him she was going to unravel any minute and he knew it. He placed his lips on hers taking her breath away and silencing her at the same time. "Must you," she smiled staring at him still inside of her.

"I must," he joked kissing her neck. "You scream and no one will sleep." He assured her noticing it was almost midnight. "I'm gonna go find something to eat. You good?"

"I'm good." She assured him smiling as she stared at his bare behind walking away. Rolling over she was comfortable for all of five seconds before her phone vibrated making her open her eyes and reach over for her phone off the nightstand. Her body ran cold at the sight of the headline on the blog.

Local Supermodel Last to See Missing Football Player, the subject read. *I haven't ran the story yet. Wanna comment?*

Gi sighed feeling her whole body tense up. "Name your price," she responded before letting the phone drop to the carpet and tightly closing her eyes struggling between irritation and exhaustion. Someone obviously didn't want her to prosper but that was a tomorrow problem.

Standing at the kitchen island Ro quietly devoured his turkey sandwich enjoying his bliss. His businesses were great, his son was healthy and in a few weeks he'd be married to his dream girl. He didn't have all that long to bask in his bliss before his phone vibrated on the counter and he sighed no longer hungry as he stared at the four pictures Austin sent him. The first three were candid photos of a healthier Alana and the fourth was a candid of Gi holding Tony with no security in sight.

Thanks for ruining my morning... Ro pressed send and shook his head from side to side in disbelief. His gold of finding the missing Monroe was getting harder especially since the person holding all the cards wasn't playing fair.

...

"Stell if Mickey's looking for me tell her I had an errand and please keep Tony for an hour."

Stella nodded staring at Anjel bouncing Tone on her lap unsure of who liked the bouncing more between the both of them. It wasn't unusual for Anje to disappear without security and very few words. *What do I tell Rome when his security notices you're not here?*

Nothin, they won't, Gi pressed send on her phone responding to Stella's text before pulling away from Gigi Boutique heading towards the coffee shop her newest extortionist had insisted they meet. Her heart pounded deep in the depths of her stomach as she was racing against the clock. No one would know she was gone if she returned within the hour. The sex tape was one thing but this was a new can of worms that needed to stay closed.

Pulling up to a very unfinished 42 Café Gi released a heavy breath of air she didn't know she was holding in. She was glad to know the café wasn't open yet so she had no pesky photographers to worry about. The sign on the door said *Opening August 30th* but the inside said otherwise. She stood in front of the shop noticing there were only two tables and four chairs and the only finished furnishing was the bookshelf line with books that wrapped around the shop and the front counter.

"Hello," Anje sang out looking around but not moving.

"Oh! Hi, Anjel," a young woman who looked no older than twenty-four greeted her walking in from the back. She had a caramel complexion, almond brown eyes and stood around 5'7". "I'm Naomi. I'm my boss's assistant. She's not coming. Her blog is important and so is her anonymity."

"What?" Anjel questioned wanting to scream but smiling instead trying to pretend to be unbothered. "Fine. I'm only handing over this check if you sign this NDA. This ain't my first rodeo. If you and your boss publish or distribute anything that harms my likeness I will sue an' I'll take the coffee shop too. It has potential." Gi spoke so polite that it was almost frightening. She handed Naomi the contract and a hot pink Gigi Boutique pen out of her purse.

"I could just release the story and say fuck the money," Naomi tapped the pen against the front counter not expecting a tense exchange.

"It will be your last story I promise you." Gi spoke staring down at the contract and then at Naomi challenging her. "I don't have all day I…"

"Aye! Ni, you seen…oh shit! Hey Gi I was just 'bout to hit you up."

Naomi froze shocked as Sean walk in and Gi looked from both of them seriously confused.

"You know ha?" Naomi scoffed not expecting their warm reunion.

"Who's this bitch? I have thirty minutes before everyone at my office runs out of lies to tell my security an' alerts my fiancé I'm gone. Who does she work for? Why she shopping around gossip about me and extorting me for money."   .

Sean stared from Naomi to Anjel and scratched at his hair knowing she didn't want the answer. "Megan. Naomi works for Meagan."

"Sign the paper Naomi," Anjel looked back at Naomi before trying to calmly speak to Sean but there was no polite way to threaten anyone. "Tell Megan that if my name comes out her mouth I will rip her vocal chords out her throat."

"She's not my girlfriend anymore. She dropped outta law school to do this and I guess blog." Sean placed his hands up needing Anje to know he had nothing to do with this. "I know what you capable of I'm just here 'cause crazy claim she pregnant. Please go back to work and calm down I know," Sean paused staring at the email exchange between Megan and Gi and the look in her eyes said it all. "Like I said we ain't together. The baby she carryin' might be mine. I'mma tell her 'bout herself. Just chill."

Gi scowled before grabbing the NDA from Naomi and storming out of the coffee shop.

Sean released a sigh of relief and glanced at a slightly frightened Naomi standing with her arms across her chest. "Gi's bite is way worse than her bark. I'd back off. Where's Megan?"

Naomi placed her hand on her chest and before she could utter a lie she was interrupted by Megan's screaming outside.

"What up bitch!"

"No,no,no," Sean rushed outside and grabbed Gi from behind. He and Meg weren't on good terms but she was very much pregnant and he vividly remembered Anje's temper.

"Let me go," Gi whined kicking as he lifted her off the ground and carried her towards her car ignoring her screams and the attention they were getting.

"You call me a cheater but a soon as some shit pop off you grab her not me. She's a whore! Gigi I don't know why these niggas flock to you."

"Gi," Sean begged putting her down and sandwiching her between him and her car.

"Sean," she whined trying to move him away.

"Please go home. I'll talk to her. She crazy as fuck."

Gi rolled her eyes staring at Meg coming their way. "I'm crazier."

"I'm sure you are. I'm not movin' 'til you calm. I know you." He spoke calmly trying to diffuse the situation.

"You callin' me a liar? They ain't stories if they true.

Gi locked eyes with Sean and placed her hands up surrendering calling a truce.

Hesitant, he backed away knowing she'd get in her car.

"You can't take the truth bitch?" Meg screamed walking past Sean and approaching Anjel. Sean reached for Megan's arm and she quickly pulled away. "I know your story."

Gi didn't let her finish. She quickly connected her fist with Megan's jaw before rolling her eyes and getting in her car and speeding off.

"Where did this come from? Why you gotta fuck with her?"

Megan grabbed at her jaw and scowled. "Because no matter what we are, I'm always competing with bitches like her."

"But you cheated! What the fuck?" He screamed confused. "Either way, this feud is dead. That's not someone you wanna fuck over!"

Meg rolled her eyes still grabbing at her jaw. "Or else what? She's like five nothing. I'll step on her. This means war…"

…

"Really," Gi groaned walking into her office from the back immediately noticing the silence. She paused noticing Ro in her chair and no Tony in his playpen.

"I've called six times and you ignored me."

"I had an errand," she assured him staring down at the desk.

"Can you look at me and say that?" He smiled knowing she was lying solely off her body language.

"Ro," she whined staring up at him. "Can you just trust me?"

"Uhh no! I was worried." He paused scratching his jaw as she stood agitated.

"I wanted to," she sighed fumbling over her words. "I wanted to handle this myself. I got an email threatening to expose that whole Todd situation and I panicked. And then I found out it was Megan and I got angry."

Ro nodded staring at her laptop screen. "And then you punched her in the face." Ro pointed at the monitor. "You gave her exactly what she wanted. Look."

Gi's face grew red at the sight of the footage of the altercation. She wasn't sure if she was more embarrassed or angry that someone invaded her privacy and everything she did was now under a microscope.

"Did this have anything to do with Sean? Just lemme know now 'cause…"

"No," she scoffed placing her hand on her hip and staring at him in disbelief. "He's not even supposed to be in town. The baby Megan's carrying might be his. That bitch lucky he was there."

"How do you spin this into positive news?" He got serious upset with the entire situation.

Gi shrugged. "You don't," she smiled thinking of how great it felt to punch Megan. "Paint me as a bad girl. I wouldn't give a shit. I'm nobody's puppet. I just wanna design clothes an' work on my empire."

"This is messy," he argued shocked by her nonchalant behavior.

"So be it! I'm tired of everyone being in my business. The next time I see her I'm gonna choke her."

"Please don't do that." Ro sighed over her theatrics. "Remember how I said to let me know if something like this happened? We're a team and I got your back but I can't when you're out there doin' shit like this… "

"I'm done for the day. You got Tone all this is draining… I love you." Gi huffed before grabbing her purse and storming out the same way she came in.

⋯

"This just in, local celebrity Gigi Monroe is trending. She got into an altercation with basketball player Sean Robinson's bae. Rumor has it those two were really close."

Li rolled her eyes before turning off the television and heading to the kitchen to find dinner.

"Ant Ann!" Dontae squealed storming out of the living room and Asia followed behind him as he raced to the front door to meet her. Asia may have gotten on her nerves at times but she was great with Tae so it didn't bother her none. It was nice to have an extra body around because at six he was becoming a handful.

"Munchkin!" Anjel's face brightened at the sight of the excitement in his eyes. "You're gonna be as big as me in a second.

Hey Asia." She acknowledged Asia not realizing she was being observed.

"Good, Anjel. You come to chat an' I'll listen but you're making dinner."

Gi shrugged holding Dontae's hand. "Wait," she let go and grabbed Li's hand and immediately scoffed shocked at the engagement ring.

"It's new like last night new. I was working on getting everyone…"

"But I'm your twin," Gi argued staring at her like she had lost her mind. "Give me the details. How he propose? When's the wedding? No you can't have my day. We already have the same birthday. What did he do to make you say yes?" Gi bubbled over with excitement.

"It's not an interesting story. I asked him why, an argument ensued, and some good advice from friends brought us to yes. Now tell me about this viral fight."

Gi rolled her eyes before giving Dontae her phone to play with in the other room so she could rehash the day's events. "I was beyond pissed. Leave a bitter Becky like Megan to wanna pull the skeletons out my closet 'cause she had Sean and she cheated."

006. Amateur Hour

"I usually wouldn't but I have a work affair coming up. How does this work?" 42-year-old Eric Ellis sat on the living room couch of the ridiculously decked out Ramsey Mansion hoping to find an escort on short notice for his MBU affair.

"Well," Nathaniel Ramsey started placing his cup on the coffee table and pulling out photo of the many escorts on his payroll. "You tell me what you're looking for, you pay me an' depending on how much money you put in my hand you get an escort to do whatever respectfully."

Eric glanced down at the head shots of the many beautiful women and froze at the sight of a young woman comfortably standing in the doorway in nothing but a white crop top and the tiniest blue jean cut offs. "How 'bout her?" He couldn't look away mesmerized by her dark brown eyes and golden brown skin that was the same gold as her hair.

Nate stared at Korrine standing in the doorway and shook his head no. "I'm sure you want something more sophisticated. She's a bit set in her ways." Nate sighed scanning through the photos. All of Korrine's clients came to the house. She was a wildcard and him and his brother rarely let her out of their sight for that very reason.

"I'm accepting an' award from my alma mater where I got my doctorate. I'm sure I can handle a feisty one. I'll give you three grand for five hours."

"That's an awful lot," Nate let his hunger for money take over as he stared at Korrine smiling a the both of them.

"She looks like a good time. You know what? This is crazy. I'll go solo."

"No, no, no. Korrine." Nate motioned her over. "Korrine meet Doctor Ellis. He's receiving an award and wants to celebrate with him. Can I trust you to do that?"

Korrine stood with a smug smirk on her face and lust in her eyes. Nate didn't care if the lust was real he just needed her on her best behavior. "I'll show you a great time an' you're right. I clean up well." She leaned in and whispered in his ear giving him the perfect view of her D cup breasts.

"Okay so it's settled."

Korrine smiled watching him get up trying to avoid eye contact on account that he was all the way turned on.

"See you at eight. I'll send you the details. Thanks Nate... Korrine." He felt like a teenage boy who just met his favorite porn star as he awkwardly waved goodbye and showed himself out.

"Korrine," Nate grabbed her face and stared in her eyes still in awe that she was serious about being sober. "Just remember the last time you ran away. You won't have to wish you were dead 'cause this time you will be." Her confident smile both annoyed and frightened him. "I don't like you but my clients fuckin' love you. Now get out of my sight."

...

"So wait a minute. You cut Ty's hours an' gave her an assistant and... you gave her a raise. Were clothes involved in this negotiation?" Bellz joked as her, Ro, Aus, and Anje sat in a noisy Club Juliet enjoying a night off. Bellz had given Marisol the assistant manager gig clearing up her free time to enjoy Kori and life in general. She loved Juliet but there was no way that it was going to become her life especially since it wasn't Rome's life.

"Clothes weren't but that girl could have the world." Aus confirmed taking a sip of his drink and smiling as another girl took the stage. Amateur night was entertaining and one of Bellz' bright ideas but it brought in crowds and kept money flowing so nobody exactly hated it.

"What have you done with Austin and where is he?" Bellz joked impressed with Tyler's hold on him. He smiled more and everyone could see she was happy. *Leave it to a woman to make him smile*, she thought to herself. Staring down at her phone vibrating she sighed staring at a short text from Kori. "I think Kori's jealous of Li. Y'all she keep askin' if we ever had a thing."

"Well have y'all?" Ro was the first to question and Gi playfully punched him in the arm as she sat on his lap.

"No! She's my best friend!" Bellz rolled her eyes completely floored he'd ask that.

"Have you ever thought about it?"

"Have you?" Bellz tilted her head over Ro's shenanigans.

"No," he admitted placing his hand on Gi's thigh watching her sip on rum and pineapple. Jan had Tone until Sunday and today was the first day of their four-day vacation and it almost felt like old times.

"Her ass is huge," Aus changed the subject as the club got louder and all eyes were glued to the woman on stage. 5'3" Tamara "Tiny" Dennis had nothing tiny on her. Men and women threw money at her as she slid down the pole and then into a split keeping the beat. The girl was made for exotic dancing. Her ass, tiny waist, and her C cups made it hard to stare into her brown eyes.

"She's been here. She showed up yesterday lookin' for a job. I told her to come to amateur night." Bellz sighed observing the girl's crowd. "She has a huge ego." Bellz placed her hand on her chin recalling their previous encounter.

"But that ass though," Aus chuckled watching her smack her own ass before the music ended and she collected her money.

"What you think?" Ro questioned staring at Gi.

"She aight! Her ass nice but her wigs a mess."

"We're sorry everyone's dad can't be whatever the hell yours was Monroe." Bellz teased making Gi laugh. "You right though. Shorty nice. I seen better." Bellz spotted Tiny out of the corner of her eye standing at the bar.

The second Gi got up to go to the bathroom Tiny saw it as her cue to approach their booth. "Will you hire me?" The name Tiny made sense as the young woman had a soft tiny voice.

"I usually wouldn't interfere but she good for business," Ro chimed in smiling at Bellz.

"He knows his business," Tiny directed her charm Ro's way hoping to entice one of them.

"Do you manage this Zoo?" Bellz cut her eyes at Rome. He gave her the power to manage the place and she had no desire to fuck up the dynamics of her club with someone who had such an inflated ego.

"I don't want...don't." Ro started and froze as Tiny planted her behind on Ro's lap.

"I wouldn't," Bellz nervously rubbed her forehead staring at Tiny gyrating her hips. "Don't," she spoke sternly cutting her eyes at Ro who put his hands up at the sight of his fiancé.

"Up, now," Gi sternly ordered scowling at the two of them. "Please un-ass my fiancé."

Tiny smiled at Gi not moving challenging her.

"Aight! You hired, please," Ro shoo-ed her knowing even a drunk Anjel wasn't one to play with.

"Really," she scoffed watching Tiny walk away while Ro was fixated on Anjel's jealousy.

"Jealousy looks good on you." Gi rolled her eyes still upset with his antics. "I'm marryin' you! Stop!" He pulled her on to his lap before refilling their glasses. "Why can't we just finish this bottle, watch strippers an' go home to a quiet house?"

She huffed picking up her glass and sipping at her champagne. "You're an asshole."

"I love you too." He planted a kiss on her cheek before staring around the table looking for an out from this conversation.

"How you Ivy free?" Aus lightened the mood and glanced Bellz' way noticing her usual shadow was MIA.

"I don't know somethin' bout a ceremony at MBU. She smart as hell an' using it as networking event. I don't' care what it is. She's a headache but I love her."

...

"Korrine you do clean up well."

Korrine got an eerie feeling in the pit of her stomach as Nate walked in her room with a giant grin on his face and a manila folder in hand. He was never happy to see her so that immediately made alarms go off in her head. She held on to her robe tightly.

"No need for the robe. I want a free sample. How good you goin' treat Mr. Fuller?"

"Whatever he wants," she assured him with a smile hoping he would go away but instead he backed her into the wall.

"Look at me!"

She stared in his big brown eyes with no trace of fear in her body. On the outside she appeared calm but inside she was dying to escape but wouldn't give him the satisfaction of seeing her weak. "You've been hidin' a secret Korrine. You disappear tonight an' I'm trading up."

She froze staring at his candid photos of Anjel. "I know where to find her. She younger, prettier and more naïve, Alana."

She smiled at the photos. It had been way too long since she'd last seen her sisters. They were once the center of her universe. Her smiled quickly faded realizing why her universe imploded. She could handle the Ramsey brothers but the question tugging at her was if Anjel could. Every worst-case scenario frightened her. Alana was reckless, Aliyah was overprotective and Anjel was always someone's prey.

"Nate, why must you…" La tried regaining her composure.

"'Cause you're a wildcard. Every time you've stepped foot out this crib you've tried to escape and I drag you back. I really wish you didn't make a lot of fuckin' money then I could strangle you."

"Leave her out of it," La insisted and he smiled happy to have leverage.

"Enjoy your date Alana Monroe."

"Fuck," she groaned watching him walk out of the room and slam the door behind him. He left the photos scattered along the bed and the knots in her stomach refused to untangle. *You got this,* she told herself staring at a smiling Anjel. "You'll figure it out. You've been through worse."

...

"You look fuckin' gorgeous. Congrats on bein' in the top three in your department. Thanks for inviting me."

Ivy smiled walking into MBU's ballroom glad to be among the smartest and wealthiest MBU students and alumni. She always told herself if she couldn't be rich, she'd at least be smart because there was nothing worse than a broke dummy.

"This is fancy," Ivy nodded grabbing Tara's hand and dragging her toward the d'oeuvres.

"No, thank you for comin' with and that dress…" Ivy smiled staring Tara down. It was almost as if her black bodycon midi dress was cut for her and Ivy couldn't wait to get her out of it.

"Ivy. My brightest pupil. I'm glad you made it."

"Dr. Fuller how could I miss it? It's not the same without you teaching here." Ivy smiled staring at her former professor all dapper and well rested.

"You'll be fine. If you need letters of recommendation or anything let me know. Oh…" Eric paused watching Korrine stroll over in a navy blue short sleeved cocktail dress that hugged the right curves and commanded attention. "Speaking of fine. Meet my dear friend Korrine. Korrine this is my former student Ivy and her friend..."

"Tara," Ivy introduced her proudly placing her hand on Tara's shoulder. "Nice to meet you Korrine." Ivy paused taking her in. She was runway gorgeous. She expected nothing less from Eric because he'd always been flashy but damn. "You have this Monroe trend down to a science. You look like you belong on The A Team." Ivy smiled admiring her golden-brown candy curled to perfection. "My sister is best friends with Anjel Monroe's twin and her boyfriend. Look."

La smiled surprisingly not irritated by her bragging. There was no doubt that Ivy was related to Isabelle who just so happened to be Aliyah's right hand. *Damn this city's small,* she thought staring at the fashion show photos. "Who's that?" she pointed pretending to be confused at the picture of Anje and Ro hugging.

"Oh," Ivy stared at Alana a bit hesitant. "That's her fiancé. He's never in the spotlight. I promised to delete it but I would never invade their privacy." Ivy immediately put her phone in her clutch hoping she hadn't said too much.

Rome and Anjel, Alana thought to herself super confused. That was all she needed to know before taking drastic measures. Gi wasn't in good hands she was in the best hands. Aliyah was overprotective, Rome was beyond it.

"Is everything okay?" Eric questioned her silence as she followed him around to work the room.

"Everything is great." She smiled and kissed him on the cheek before helping herself to another glass of wine. The more they worked the room, the more she observed Ivy. That had to be her in. She couldn't just swipe Ivy's phone and call Bellz to call Li because it wasn't efficient and for all she knew Nate had someone watching Anjel at this very moment. She needed something calculated and that wouldn't blow up in her face.

"Get in the photo with us." Eric waved her over insisting she'd sandwich him between her and Ivy. For once her smile was real. She didn't mind his hand on the nape of her back or when he hugged her just a little too tight to make his colleagues jealous. She had a plan and was content with all the worst-case scenarios.

"I'll be back," she whispered following Ivy and Tara to the bathroom. Her eyes widened amused by Ivy's giggling as her and Tara fooled around in the stall. Swiftly she grabbed Ivy's phone out of the black and gold clutch on the sink. She wasn't going to go to her sisters. She was going to bring them to her. Three Monroe sisters were always stronger than one.

. . .

"A whole weekend no work? You don't need downtime. You make babies in your downtime."

Gi playfully rolled her eyes smiling at Mickey standing in her office with an advanced copy of the latest issue of B Magazine. "My trainer could ask me for the world," Gi joked admiring her half naked spread promoting her denim line.

"What we ohh-ing at?" Ro interrupted their celebrating standing in the doorway with a smile. "What happened to no surprises?" His eyes widened and face grew red at the magazine in Mickey's hand.

"I sell lingerie." Gi raised her brow not here for him raining on her parade. "Why are you here? You had me the entire weekend."

"Cake tasting," he smiled giddy about the wedding and Gi shook her head recalling the drunk conversation about cake.

"Drunk me made that appointment lemme grab my things. Give me a second."

"A second Gi," he insisted following Mickey towards the front impressed by his fiancé's hustle.

"Does the name Alana Korrine Monroe mean anything?" Mickey quietly stopped him pulling in the hallway dividing the store and the office space.

"It depends what," Ro started and paused as Mickey handed him the phone displaying the email from Ivy's email address.

Alana Korrine Monroe
6359 Cambria Drive
--- xo I've never given up

"You ain't mention this to Gi," he quietly questioned sending himself the address before handing her the phone.

"No, it it's not a photoshoot or a runway, I don't bother with it. We'd never get anything done. Should I be concerned?" Mickey pocketed the phone and slowly walked towards the back exit.

"No, you're good. Tell her to hurry up. Thanks Mick."

007. Seeing Ghosts

"So, the plan is you just show up lookin' for her. This place isn't a drive. It's on its own street. It's a fuckin' castle." Aus sat in the office of Club Juliet with Rome trying to find some kind of plan to act on this lead.

"It's a brothel." Marisol pipped in recognizing the luxurious Ramsey Mansion. It was one of many but this one was a nightmare. "It's the Ramsey Mansion. On the outside it's nice, inside is a nightmare."

"No fuckin' way," Rome shook his head. "How you know?"

"It's an escort service," Marisol placed emphasis on her words with sarcasm as heavy as her accent. "Lots of those women were trafficked or came here from very fucked up situations. Ramsey's trade up and umm sometimes take women from other escort services. It's a brothel. I've never been but heard stories."

"You can't stay away from this place?" Aus joked cutting the awkward silence happy to see Bellz and fill her in.

"I could ask y'all the same. Y'all need jobs." Bellz chuckled staring around the room and shaking her head at Ro and Aus who were obviously bored of being just owners.

"Ivy accidentally found La and…"

Bellz pulled out her phone and silenced them with a photo of Ivy and Alana who were having the time of their lives with champagne flutes in hand. "Yeah she did. That tattoo is so fuckin' ugly. I remember when she got it." Bellz zoomed in on the small spider caught in the web on the right side of Alana's neck. Remembering La trying to explain that the web was life and she was the spider. "La is goin' by Korrine. Apparently, she was there with one of Ivy's old professors. None of this makes sense."

"Ever heard of the Ramsey twins?" Marisol pulled up a photo of Nathaniel and Nicholas Ramsey surrounded in a sea of women.

"Uhh yeah. They own half the town making bank off flippin' property."

"They're also buying and selling women. Trading them like sports cards." Marisol sighed thinking about how fucked up the situation was.

"Apparently, La swiped Ivy's phone and emailed the address to Gi." Aus connected it for her confirming Bellz' worst case scenario.

"So La's really in some shit?" Bellz stood appalled not knowing what to do now that the air was clear.

"She's not exactly living the dream," Ro assured her looking through the photos.

"We can't just show up lookin' for her," Aus thought out loud.

"Where my party invite at? Uhh." The room grew quiet as Dyce walked in and froze as if he saw a ghost. "That's the reckless Monroe."

"It is. She been missin' so long we guessed she was dead." Aus explained.

"What if I go lookin' for a night." Bellz sat back trying to find a way to reach Alana.

"No, we don't need your fine ass disappearing. They might take you." Ro semi-joked. "I'll go with Dyce. We can say we shooting a video at Karma. It's believable. I ain't had no fun in a minute."

"Your sister-in-law and fiancé will kill you if you fuck this up." Bellz sighed slightly jealous that their night was going to be way more exciting than hers.

"You can't say nothin'." Everyone looked at Bellz knowing how strong her allegiance to Li was.

"I'll be here all night. I can't lie if I'm busy."

"Why are you even here? I thought it was my night?" Marisol placed her hand on her hip and stood over Bellz was confused.

"Long story me and Kori had a little argument but my drama is nothin' compared to this."

This is crazy…

Bae: Jerome Christopher, you sent me to voicemail why? -_-

Ro smiled putting down his phone ignoring Gi's text before following Dyce out of the car and towards the entry of the Ramsey Mansion. Even in the night time the house was a work of art. Pictures didn't do this castle any justice.

"Hey fellas, how may I help you?" Upon ringing the doorbell, they were greeted by a young woman who looked not a day over twenty-five. She looked more like a model than someone who was being held captive.

"We don't have appointments but me..."

"You're Dyce Kennedy," she interrupted Rome and ushered the two of them into the foyer.

"Yeah! I'm putting together this video shoot last minute and a great friend, Eric Fuller recommended your services."

She smiled with lust in her eyes staring Dyce down. "Stay here. I'll go get the boss and see what we can do." She winked before sashaying away in her tiny black shorts and white crop top.

They didn't even have a chance to snoop around before Nicholas Ramsey approached them hiding his excitement to see Dyce Kennedy. All his music videos look like legendary parties and here he was looking for girls. "What can I do for you? Do you have a type? How many hours?"

"About five hours, no touchin', uhh. I need four girls an' that chic that was on Eric Fuller's arm. She hot. Real Gigi Monroe like." Dyce smiled rubbing at his chin.

"You don't want her. I." Nick paused watching Dyce pull a wad of money out of his pocket.

"That's my type. That's two stacks right there. I'll give you the rest tonight at Karma at 8pm, it's goin' be live."

Nick nodded grabbing the money and dapping Dyce up. "Pleasure doing business with you. Hope we can make this a thing."

"Pleasures all mine. You're a fuckin' lifesaver."

Both Rome and Dyce smiled discreetly looking around as they followed Nick to the front door.

"Was that crazy or what?" Dyce was the first to speak as he started the car.

"Insane," Ro agreed releasing a heavy sigh as his phone lit up flashing a picture of him and Gi. "Yes," politely he greeted her. "You don't even want nothin. I'm busy. Come to Karma tonight and 8. It's closed. I'll explain later an' yeah I work. Love you too."

"I can't believe that place is a fuckin' brothel." Dyce was still amazed as he stopped at the red light.

"This is crazy but it better be the real deal or I'm out of two stacks and all the Monroes will kill me."

Dyce chuckled seeing the nervous expression on Ro's face. "They sure will. Those girls will eat you alive."

...

"We're late! Please stop crying." Gi pleaded with Tony cursing him under breath as she placed a pacifier in his mouth and unbuckled him from his car seat. *I'm sure he hates me as much as I hate him.* She told herself carrying him towards a very empty Karma. "Antonio," she groaned beyond frustrated watching the pacifier fall to the ground and he began crying again. "Ugh," She huffed leaning over and picking the pacifier up.

"Yo! Your husband to be lookin' for you. Go check 'em out." Dyce stood at the front door of Club Karma surprised to see a frazzled Anjel.

"Where's your phone?" An equally annoyed Rome was the first to greet her.

"I'm late because he won't stop crying. I can't hear myself think. You take him 'cause I'mma cry if he doesn't stop."

"Gi," he started and smiled as Tony grew quiet as soon as he picked him up.

"Why are we here?" Li stole the words out of Gi's mouth and the two of them froze watching four girls walk into Karma. Three of them were invisible to the two of them as their eyes immediately caught sight of the oldest Monroe. Li's voice tangled in her throat as tears of joy filled her eyes.

"Am I," Gi tilted her head questioning her vision.

"You're not." Aliyah finished her thought watching Alana strut over shocked at their reunion. "La," Aliyah flung her arms around her sister and Gi's smile widened joining in.

"You were very hard to track down." Ro interrupted their reunion and Alana smiled at him holding what had to be the youngest Monroe.

"Thank you," quietly she spoke staring back at Gi and Li behind her. "But I can't stay."

"Why?" Both Anje and Li questioned confused to what they were missing and why La was trying to be quiet about leaving.

"Where did you find her?" Li's happiness turned into a slight panic realizing people didn't just disappear for two years.

"I got caught up. Too many enemies. I didn't leave that hospital willingly."

"You couldn't have. We saw you." Gi agreed placing her hand on her hip trying to piece together what happened. "Where have you been?"

"The guy that tried to kill me came back and instead of finishing the job he did the opposite. He nursed me back to health and instead made me wish he'd killed me." Alana paused pushing a stray strand of hair behind her ear. "Long story short I was prostituted and then trafficked eventually I ended up at The Ramsey's high end escorting. I've been telling people my name is Korrine. They threatened if I didn't return they'd go after Anje."

Gi rolled her eyes and smiled at Alana who had risked her life numerous times for her. "Trust me. You can't go back. I've dealt with worse an' Ro here is marrying me. He doesn't let me out of his sight. You're ours now." Gi smiled from ear to ear refusing to take no for an answer.

"What are you gonna do then cause those fuck boys mean business.?"

Gi huffed like a child shocked to see a vulnerable Alana. "Look at me," she placed her finger underneath her chin. "I don't care what happened in the past or who screwed you over. You're home now."

"You're Gigi Monroe." Gi nodded scrunching up her face confused by the two strange men wandering towards them.

"We're closed," she politely informed the two men. Her smile widened as they flashed police badges. "What in the actual world." She spoke under her breath meeting them halfway trying not to attract attention.

"We're investigating Nathaniel and Nicholas Ramsey. We've reason to believe you or someone at this establishment purchased…"

Gi shook her head objecting. "I assure you there's a misunderstanding. Let's take this conversation outside where it's much quieter." She didn't have to look back to know Rome was following her. She was always on his radar as if he GPS chipped her. "It's not what it looks like. The women you are investigating."

"We're investigating Nicholas and Nathaniel prostitution ring. You," the taller one stood skeptical waiting for an explanation.

"We didn't purchase sex. That's creepy. One of the girls has been missing for years. She's my sister. We thought she was dead." Gi sighed. "I've never seen her so terrified in my life."

"Would she testify in court?" His partner questioned standing next to him intrigued by the whole situation.

"Probably not. Why do you need her? They're sayin' they run an escort service. It's not true. The girls are victims." Rome filled in the blanks standing behind her with a very quiet Tony.

"We know that we're raiding their mansion as we speak. We saw four girls leave and were obligated to follow. Especially since money was exchanged."

"We were trying to do the right thing. You have dozens of girls to testify Let's forget this one exists please." Ro was impressed at how well she was handling this. "I don't know what state she's in. We lost her years ago. We'll take her to the hospital to check her out. I wanna see the Ramsey's rot. Did you propose I approached them asking to see my sister? Technically no laws were broken. No sex will be had with any of those women. We purchased their freedom in the midst of your raid."

"Can we interrogate her?" The taller one questioned a bit sympathetic as their intentions were pure.

"Another time tomorrow. Here's my card." Anje handed the officer a hot pink business card elated to watch them walk away.

"Since Li has Asia we'll take La. She can sleep on the couch."

"Whatever you say." Ro agreed kissing her on her forehead.

. . .

"Are you excited? In a few days, you'll officially be Mrs. Jones."

Gi smiled from ear to ear twirling around in her white short sleeved, scoop neck lace overlay mermaid fit dress that hugged every curve just right. "Bellz," she paused staring around at Bellz sandwiched in between Li, Tyler, Ivy and Asia as the five of them sat on the couch in the dressing room entertained at the fact that they had received complimentary champagne because Gi wanted to try on her wedding dress one last time. What was supposed to be everyone picking up their dresses turned into an impromptu afterhours bridal party. "Am I excited? Yeah! Now Ro can stop asking me when you goin' be my wife? I swear no one's more excited than him. He's like my little my little groom-zilla!"

"What y'all goin' argue about then?" Li joked tapping her nails against the plastic champagne flute.

"Who knows? This guy has this whole fairytale in his head." Gi spun around again admiring her reflection in the mirror. "He does mean well even when he goes overboard. This dress is bomb." Gi looked back over her shoulder posing in the mirror.

"It better be," Li laughed. "Especially for the price tag."

Gi rolled her eyes at her twin and scoffed. "You only get married once."

"My point exactly! You better parade around in that thing or get buried in it."

Gi shook her head before heading towards the back to slip back into her previous outfit. It all seemed surreal to her. She was finally going to get her happily ever after that she so badly deserved. "What about you plus one?" Gi returned in wedding planning mode and stood in front of Bellz finally addressing Kori's absence.

"Here's a glass and Ivy is my plus one. Ivy's not bringing her boyfriend or her girlfriend."

Gi nodded not bothering to pry and slightly intrigued by Ivy's life.

"You have a boyfriend and a girlfriend?" Tyler leaned over questioning how she had missed this information.

"I've had boyfriends and girlfriends. I'm not attracted to gender I'm attracted to people."

"My parents weren't exactly religious but they would've told me I needed Jesus if I came home and told them that." Tyler sipped at her champagne curious to how Ivy and Bellz parents dealt with their daughters' sexualities.

"So you're telling me," Ivy leaned in towards Tyler and placed her glass on the coffee table. "If Dallas came home one day and said she was interested in boys and girls you wouldn't even try to understand."

Tyler sat back on the couch and sighed before staring back over towards Ivy. "I don't know. I just want her to stay cute forever. That's a touchy situation."

"Is Alana coming to the wedding?" Bellz was the first to change the subject knowing Ivy's free spirited ways were probably a lot to comprehend to some people.

"Yes, Alana is coming but she said being there is great enough and she doesn't have to be in it."

"She seems a bit off." Aliyah huffed staring at Gi reading the hint of disappointment on her face.

"She'd have to be on for us to know she was off. She's been through a lot and she raised us. Whatever she's going through I'm down for the ride because that's what we do."

"Cheers to that!" Ivy yelled raising her glass for a toast.

"Cheers to that!" Liyah repeated.

...

"Where's Gi? What time is it?" Alana sat up on the couch and stretched her arms staring at Rome holding Tony in his arms.

"Trying on her dress one last time before the big day and it's noon. You got somewhere to be?" Ro smiled semi-joking.

"No. No just wondering. He looks like your twin. It's ridiculous." She smiled staring at Tony eating his hand.

"She a bit of a hurricane. She was goin' wake you up and see if you wanted to go but I told her to let you sleep."

"Yes. That's the best sleep I've had in a long time." Alana sat smiling at Tony stuck on how precious he was. "How you turn my sister into little Susie homemaker?"

"I didn't. I'm living in the Anjel Show. We all just tryna get a leading role." He joked taking a seat on the ottoman across from Alana.

"He looks like a clone of the both of you. It's sickening. I've missed so much."

"We can't change the past but we have now."

"Tell me 'bout this Asia chick."

"Anthony was a rolling stone. Li met her at the hospital. Asia lost her daughter in a shootout. She stays with Li, works with Gi and from what I gather they stay out of each other's way. Asia is all I wanna know 'bout my father and Gi's all I met him he was an asshole."

"Well she not lying. I'll never forget her covered in his blood on the kitchen floor. She was innocent til she wasn't. I still don't see how little ol' her found the strength to stab that man about nine times. She blamed him for Korrine. Why are you marrying her?"

"She's the real thing. Somehow she makes me the best version of myself and I don't want to lose that so I keep her close."

"She's definitely a gem." La smiled staring around at their family pictures on the mantel above the fireplace. "I just knew I'd be married with kids and a bit settled by now." She sighed repositioning herself so she was sitting Indian style on the couch. "I've endured hell and now I believe in karma."

Rome silently stared at her knowing there was more and knowing sometimes silence was the best way to get someone to talk.

"I'm pregnant." Was not the words he assumed she would blurt out.

"You're what?" He grew concerned raising his brow. "By who?"

"Nicholas Ramsey." She leaned back and stared at the ceiling before bringing her attention back to Ro. "You can't tell anyone I'm still processing this all and I don't need any of my drama overshadowing this wedding."

"Gi's not excited about the wedding. She just wants to get away for this honeymoon." Ro paused knowing he couldn't ignore what she had just told him. "I'll keep your secret until after the wedding."

"Fair enough. Thanks for never giving up on me and always being there no matter how drastic it is."

"We're family. That's what family does. Try to stay out of trouble please."

Alana smiled thinking about the past her and realizing that girl was long gone. "I have no trouble to get into."

"I'm sure with our many establishments nowadays. We'll find you a job to keep you occupied. Everything is gonna work out fine."

008. Karma

"Do you Anjel Monroe take Jerome Jones to be your lawful wedded husband, to have and to hold from this day forward, for better, for worse, for richer, for poorer, in sickness and health, until death do you part?"

"I do," Anje smiled admiring the view from their beachfront honeymoon rental. She stared down at the huge clear-cut pink hued rock on her finger that sparkled in the moonlight and then back at a fast-asleep Jerome. She vowed forever with him and on day three of their seven-day getaway she hoped that they could stay this way forever. Them on their own little island where time stood still, no work, no baby and no worries; that's when they were at their best.

Anjel Christine Jones kind of had a ring to it. She sighed stepping out on the balcony basking in her happily ever after. She deserved this.

"Why you up," she was so caught up in her thoughts she didn't even hear Ro get out of bed.

"Just enjoying the view and all this."

He placed a kiss on her forehead and stood behind her looking at the waves crashing on the beach. "This is kind of dope but I got the best view for the rest of my life."

"You do," she teased turning around and smiling at him before flinging her arms around his waist. "I'm glad you got me away for the week Mr. Jones. We needed this. The world won't stop while we enjoy our success."

"I'm glad you finally see that. We good. Shit ain't been this nice in so long."

They stood there, grinning enjoying each other's embrace.

"You're stuck with me now Mrs. Jones. For better or for worse."

"It better be for better," she playfully threatened.

"Hopefully better. I always got your back."

Gi closed her eyes taking him in. "Yeah 'cause now I have two big sisters watching my back."

"We good," Ro assured her. "How 'bout we just enjoy now." He placed a kiss on her lips before she could respond and Gi smiled eyes bright as he slid her robe off. The balcony was probably the only surface she hadn't had sex in the house.

We're on our forever shit…

This place is a gold mine, Tyler smiled locking up the money from the night in the lockbox in her desk drawer. She didn't know what she did to deserve Karma but she appreciated it. Staring at her family photos on her desk made her smile widen. Her and Aus weren't married but she could see herself years from now planning her wedding. Her and Austin were so different but so similar in many ways beyond not liking guacamole and practically being orphans.

Be home soon, locking up now love you :)

She sent Austin a text before grabbing her purse and heading out the office. She locked the door, hit the lights, set the alarm and in usual fashion she stood at the exit for a few seconds once outside mentally going over her closing checklist. "What," she started looking around for what sounded like someone's phone vibrating. She shrugged it off and quickly walked to her car. She placed her hand on the door and froze as she heard footsteps behind her. Quietly and swiftly she grabbed at the door handle and as soon as she went to open it the person behind her placed her hand on it.

She had closed many times without an issue and inside she was panicked. Silently she stood there praying that this person wanted money or her car. The stranger placed her hand on her head pushing it against the driver's side window to keep her from turning around.

"If you want money it's yours, whatever you want." Ty closed her eyes uncomfortable with head being pressed against the window. Her heart stopped feeling something placed against the back of her head. "You don't have to," Ty started assuming it was a gun and the stranger briefly moved her hand from her head before Tyler's head collided with the driver's seat door and Tyler's body fell limp against the concrete. The last she heard was a quiet giggle and a loud bang.

. . . .

"Ty," Aus groaned at the sound of Dallas' whining down the hallway. They didn't need an alarm because at 7AM on a daily Dallas was up whether anyone else wanted her to be. "Ty," he reached over to an empty bed and froze before quickly getting up and staring out the bedroom window overlooking the driveway. "Shit," he stood shocked that Tyler's car wasn't there. "Where," picking up his phone he called Tyler's phone for it to ring over and over again.

Hey you've reached Tyler. Sorry I'm not near my phone right now but if you leave your name and your number I may give you a call back.

He rubbed at his forehead as he made his way to Dallas' room. Relief filled his mind as Tori's name popped up on his screen and that relief quickly subsided.

"Tyler's gone! Possibly fuckin' dead! Karma, now!" Tori spoke sternly and as calm as she could.

Aus held his daughter tightly in one hand and his phone with the other. He had no idea what happened to the mother of his child. He just knew it couldn't be good.

"Da-da," Aus felt a very moment of bliss staring in his daughter's brown eyes. It just sucked that his kid's first words would be remembered as the day her mother disappeared. "Da-da," she smiled oblivious to how cruel the world could be.

"Yes, da-da's here. I'm not goin' anywhere," he promised kissing her forehead.

Home, now, Tyler's gone! Austin couldn't form a complete sentence but he knew Rome would cut his honeymoon short no questions asked.

The love of his life was gone again and this one hadn't disappeared by choice. "Please don't be dead," he silently prayed gathering Dallas' things together. "We need you."

...

"Look on the bright side we got to spend a whole three days in paradise."

Gi sighed resting her chin on his bare chest as the two of them comfortably lay in bed enjoying the last moments of their short-lived honeymoon. It was blowing her mind that their world couldn't sit still for a week while they were gone. This was the most peaceful he'd ever been. No baby, no work and just the two of them in a two-story beach front vacation rental that cost more than some people's mortgages. Mickey got her the deal of a lifetime by agreeing to post about the place after she was gone. "Who would take Tyler? She never does anything to anybody." Gi finally addressed the elephant in the room. "What are we dealin' with?"

Ro stared in her eyes sensing the worry in her face. He smiled refusing to show that he was just as unsure. "You of all people know you don't have to be into this street shit to be involved in the streets and it'll be good. We'll be good." He promised staring in her eyes. "I promise to make this trip up to you when shit die down if you promise to stop dodging my security."

Gi placed her cheek on his chest and closed her eyes trying to ignore his last demand.

"Gi," he groaned.

"They're so serious all the time. They smoother me."

"No, they protect you and I pay them a lot to do it. Let them do their job Mrs. Jones."

She smiled feeling him grab her bare behind.

"That has a nice ring to it. Mr. Jones. It's our last night in paradise. What do you wanna do?"

"Maybe find some clothes, eat dinner and if you're on your best behavior maybe you'll be dessert."

Gi chuckled opening her eyes. "I'm always on my best behavior. It's everyone else I swear."

Ro smiled amused by her argument. Good wasn't exactly her thing but that's what he enjoyed about her.

… Get you a girl that can do both…

"Aye! That's bomb. Vacay did you well. You all glowing and shit."

Gi smiled from ear to ear as Gotti showered her with compliments as soon as she stepped on set in her hot pink retro one piece that read *Angel* in white lettering. B Magazine was ringing her phone as soon they got word her honeymoon was over. She wasn't happy it got cut short but business was business and the bright side for her was she got the chance to make the cover of B Magazine with Gotti promoting their new single and her swim line dropping in the spring.

"That ring though." He admired her pink clear-cut diamond in awe.

"I'm a little spoiled I can't help it." She admired it herself standing next to him with her hand on his shoulder. It felt good to be on the cover with him and this time she wasn't a prop.

"That's good, stay there." The photographer yelled. "Now, Gi drop your arm…move closer. Gotti that's perfect."

Gotti smiled standing next to her in swim shorts. He wrapped his arm around Gi's shoulder as if they had been friends forever. The space Gi had placed between them was gone.

"I want one more sit on the edge of the pool."

The two of them did as directed and by the end they were side by side foot in the water comfortable as hell. It was crazy. How much direction wasn't necessary. The photographer just snapped away.

"You tryna hit up Mae's after this?"

Gi smiled getting up from the edge of the pool. "Flattering but no. My husband doesn't know I left. My babysitter is covering me. I just knew I had to be a part of this."

"Let me buy you a congrats on your marriage dinner," Gotti pushed.

"Ro's made progress with us working together. Let's not push it. See you Friday for the video release."

"Fo sho! Text me when you get in so I know you good."

Gi rolled her eyes appalled by his overprotective demeanor. "You sound like him."

. . .

"Have you slept? Did you even leave?" Bellz walked into Tyler's office at Karma shocked to see Victoria seated at Ty's desk glued to the surveillance on the computer screen. "Tori...honey." Bellz pulled up a chair next to her trying to tread lightly on the topic of Tyler's disappearance.

"There's six cameras outside. We missed something." Tori palmed her face and leaned in closer to the screen. "None of this makes any fuckin' sense."

Great, it's a party, Bellz thought to herself as a very intoxicated Austin and Rome stumbled in with bottles in hand. As the two of them sat down it was apparent that Bellz was the most emotionally stable person in the room. "What's up?" She questioned not expecting much of an answer from anyone.

"Victoria," Dyce walked in before either Ro or Aus could form an answer. "You still here? You ain't moved. This ain't healthy. Let's go home." Dyce stood in the center of the office trying to get Tori's attention.

"I've tried." Bellz leaned back in her chair and stared over at the footage on the screen.

"Victoria," he walked closer standing directly on the other side of the desk ignoring everyone else's' presence.

"Wow! The gangs all here. Y'all got Marisol working like a slave. What's goin' on here? No one wants to work or work on Tyler's disappearance?" Aliyah stood still trying to get a feel for the room confused to what she had walked in to. Everyone was hard to read with the exception of Tori who was so focused on the computer screen she could ignore an earthquake.

"Okay, Tori babe," Dyce tried reasoning with Tori as she clicked the buttons on the mouse. It felt like everyone in the room was on their own cloud. "Bellz, help me out here." Dyce stared at her and she placed her hands up trying to stay out of it.

"Aus. How you holding up?" Li finally brought her attention to a very drunk Austin seated next to a just as drunk Jerome.

"I'm good. I just needa know. Not knowing is hard."

Li palmed her face realizing the emotions in the room were so intense that the wrong words could send everyone off the edge. Everyone had the same emotions but no one but Bellz and Tori wanted to talk about them.

"Finally, nobody's answering their phones. I'm late for an appointment. You," Alana huffed walking into the room with Tony on her hip and distraught look on her face. "Here's your nephew." She handed Tony to Li after assessing how drunk Ro was.

"Wait," Ro's words stopped her before she could even turn around to leave. "Why you got my son? Where my wife?"

La scrunched up her face not thinking either of those questions were important. "Where's Dallas?" She brought her attention to Aus hoping to sidetrack the both of them.

"No, I'm drunk. That's not a answer." Aus sat back on the couch staring at the ceiling. "Asia watch her."

"Jerome let's not," La brought her attention to the two of them not wanting to have this conversation right now. "Let's wait til you're sober."

"Alana Korrine," Ro groaned irritated by her refusal to answer his questions. "My wife payin' you to babysit? After I specifically said no nanny."

"Monroes don't throw each other under the bus." La stared at him pleading for an out with no intention of lying to either of them.

"Alana really? You're livin' in my house. What up?"

"I'm not lying to either of you. I'm not in this."

Aus shook his head before staring at Alana in confusion. "She payin' you more than a stack?"

La stood firmly in front of them with her arms folded not saying a word.

"Two," he inquired reading her body language.

"I'm not. I'm leaving." La huffed rolling her eyes at Aus.

"Damn! Weekly or monthly?" An' if you're here. Where she at?" Aus took her abrupt need to leave as a yes and had to know more.

"She's working Ro and this is between y'all. Also, Li, he's kind of fussy and Gi's not answering. He got a little cough." La brought her attention to Li holding her nephew and sighed turning around and glancing at an irritated Ro. "Get your life Ro. Y'all both can't be drunks. Why y'all this gone and it's like three?"

"Tori let's come back to this tomorrow. You need sleep." Dyce took matters into his own hands and placed his hand over hers on the computer mouse. "Let's just." Tori sat back silently trying her hardest to digest that her best friend could be in a ditch dead on the side of some dark road never to be found. She released a heavy sigh before staring up at him towering over her and quietly exiting without looking around the room to say goodbye. Any other time Ro and Alana's bickering would've been entertaining but she didn't have the energy to laugh or argue.

"Asia watches Dal out of the kindness of her heart." Aus teased and Alana rolled her eyes through with the two of them, "Y'all should be more like Asia."

"Wait a second," Li froze glancing up at the computer screen.

"What," La walked over to her sitting there staring at the surveillance still that Tori left up on the screen. Li enlarged the photo while bouncing Tony on her lap realizing how spoiled he was.

"Look," Li pointed to the lower back tattoo exposed as the aggressor placed a hand up to grab Tyler.

"Oh shit!" Alana froze leaning over Bellz and covering her mouth as the still image of the suspect's tattoo got clearer. "I know that tattoo. You gotta be fuckin' kiddin' me."

"We know you know that tattoo." Aliyah spoke staring at her sister. "That's Rayna ain't it?"

"Didn't she used to be your best friend?" Aus smiled remembering the name.

"Weren't you and Ro fuckin' her?" La questioned with a hint of attitude.

"Whatever happened to Rayna?" Everyone in the room stared at La questioning why Rayna would do something this drastic.

"She took the fall for some work."

"And," Ro read the worry on her face and knew there had to be more to it.

"How was I supposed to know that the DA was gonna make an example of her? The DA wanted the entire squad and Ray didn't say word. I immediately cut all ties with her when I found out she was fuckin' my dude. It was a win-win for me."

"Uhh! Except it's not," Li was the first to correct her.

"She was your best friend. She wasn't exactly stable."

"Ty's probably not dead. Ray's probably lookin' for attention. I taught her everything she knows. I'd probably use Ty as bait. She doesn't know you guys know it was her. Do something to get her attention."

"Like," Li started realizing this wasn't going to end well.

"She has a sister. Grab her and offer a trade…uhh." La sighed staring down at her watch. "I'm running late."

"Where you goin' you don't have a life." Ro semi-joked taking another swig of cognac.

"Were you an' Aus really fuckin' Rayna?" Li smiled at them as she waved Alana off.

"We was young… and reckless," Aus answered for the both of them before breaking into a fit of laughter.

"Were," Li laughed shaking her head the both of them. They were probably going to have the biggest hangovers of their life.

. . .

"Monroe," Doctor Oliva Andrews called her back with a smile on her face admiring her beauty. "Your parents have strong genes. You all look alike."

"We get that a lot." Alana didn't feel into small talk but it was a well-needed distraction. She had always dreamed of being a mom just not like this.

"Alright. Up on the table and we'll see how the baby is doing."

La did as she was told and sucked in a huge breath imagining what this would've been like for her if she had a healthy relationship with the kid's father.

"Okay. Everything is fine. Baby looks healthy. Do you wanna know the sex?" Dr. Andrews smiled at Alana before staring up at the screen. "That's your little boy."

Before this very appointment, the fact that she was pregnant hadn't felt real. "I'm having a son?" She spoke quietly looking in the doctor's eyes.

"Yes, and you're both healthy. You can wait here while I got your sonogram."

Alana smiled slowly sitting up and hopping off the table. This was surreal. She had assumed that her weight gain was from her decision to be sober and all this time it was a fuckin' baby. She couldn't screw this kid up any more than she was so the bar was already high. *Dinner at Gi's at 7PM. Plz be there. I'm cooking.* She pressed send figuring it was the right time to tell her sisters her situation and what better way than to get the Monroe girls together.

"Oh my! You're gorgeous!"

The smile on Alana's face quickly faded as she watched the older woman walk in showering her with compliments.

"You're very hard to track down Alana. I mean no harm but when I heard you were carryin' my grandchild I just had to meet you. I'm Nia."

She had seen pictures of her but never actually met Nia and she was just as stunning in person. Her jet-black short bob was perfect and her red lipstick was just as precise. 52-year-old Nia Ramsey always looked photo op ready.

"You're having my grandson." Nia smiled placing the sonogram on the counter.

"What do you want?" La was hesitant to ask knowing there was no way she just wanted to meet. "I won't testify. I haven't said a word."

Nia nodded taking a seat next to her. "I need you to say that my son's ran an escort service and the girls turned it into prostitution without their knowledge."

"If I refuse?" She raised her brow in no way interested in helping the Ramsey Family. "Before you threaten me. Your children put me through hell. There is nothing you could do to me that they haven't done."

"Those boys are my pride and joy. If you do this for me I'll make sure they stay away from you an' your son."

"With al do respect Miss Ramsey. If your kids are in jail that's guarantee that they'll stay away from me."

Nia's smile dropped as she turned her body towards Alana. "If you do this one thing I will pay you monthly so you never have to work again. I'm sorry my kids are assholes but they're all I have."

"I'm gonna wake up every day with a reminder of a time when I was broken. Moneys not gonna make that better."

"It'll make it easier. If you do not help me I'll pay one of the others to do it but there's no promise that Nick will stay away.

La rolled her eyes not fazed by her threats.

"I will show up every month until you say yes."

Part of her wanted to take the deal and parade her story around but she couldn't fathom being put on the stand in either fashion. "I don't need your money. I'm fine. I'm not testifying on anyone's behalf. Drag me into a courtroom and I will plead the fifth. I just want to be alone."

"How would the media feel knowing Gigi Monroe's sister was an escort?"

La sat back and shrugged. "We can find out and drag both our family names through the mud but I wouldn't recommend it."

"Alana," Nia scoffed shocked that Alana feared nothing. "That kid will never grow up with a father."

Alana nodded. "I can live with that. He's half Monroe and half Ramsey. I'm sure he'll be fine."

"What can I..."

"Nothing," Alana stood to her feet through with the circular conversation.

"Why are you like this? I just need." Nia tried pleading and Alan shook her head with no sympathy.

"Life made me this way. Goodbye Miss Ramsey."

. . .

Sitting back in the warm water she felt like she could conquer the world. The silence of no one home felt like heaven. Staring at the bubbles she felt herself becoming one with them. She needed this. The solitude. No La, no Mickey, no Rome and most of all, no Tony.

Opening her eyes her peaceful solitude came to a screeching halt at the sight of Ro quietly leaning against the doorway obviously drunk. "Hey you," she greeted him hiding the fact that she was annoyed. He had been drunk seventy-five percent of the time they'd been home. "Is everything okay?" Her cheerful genuine concern confused him.

"Can you put clothes on? I need," Ro paused watching her stand up and grab her towel.

"I was comfy. You're home early."

Rome stood staring her down as she bent over to dry her golden-brown hair. "I need to talk to you, we…"

"Are you okay? I feel like this drinking thing isn't you? You can barely stand. Let's talk later and…"

"Where's Tony," quietly he questioned staring in her eyes as she wrapped the towel around her. "Where you been?"

"Let's talk when you're sober." She smiled hoping he'd move from the doorway and let her through.

"Let's talk now!"

"Please move," she interrupted staring him in his hazel eyes pleading him to drop it.

"Gi," he sighed standing his ground. "We gotta talk about it."

"Not right now!" Sternly she spoke placing her hand on his chest trying to push him away.

"We said no nanny and I can count on one hand the amount of times you've been here for our son. You so afraid of being a terrible mom that you don't even fuckin' try."

Quietly she stood stunned realizing he was doing this now. She raised her brow realizing this was happening and there was nothing she could do to avoid this confrontation. "One of us has to work! Especially if you're gonna continue this charade."

"Not bein' there is worse Gi. It's real fucked up!"

Gi froze giving up on getting through. She folded her arms across her chest and stared at him as if he'd struck every nerve in her body. He'd peeled her mental scab before she could even attempt to conceal it. "Well excuse me for almost dying! Not just losing a son. My son was fuckin' murdered an' less than a year later we're pregnant." Gi paused holding back tears and trying to keep herself from choking on the air in her throat. "I just wanted you. I wasn't ready for all this. I never got to grieve and every time I see him I think of that night I lost a huge part of me on a bathroom floor covered in blood. I love Tony. I just can't..." Gi paused feeling herself suffocating on her tears from the inside.

"No, you're not trying and you're not listening to yourself," he argued disappointed with the direction of this conversation.

"I really liked life before Tony."

"If your shitty excuse for parents can love you..."

"They didn't though," Gi cried coming to terms with it.

"Oh! Okay, You're bein' fuckin' dramatic. You'd rather pay your sister a lot of money than be a mom. Me an' Tone are a package deal. No Tone, no me...stop the fuckin' madness." He refused to accept her answer not caring for anything less than *I'll try harder* or an *I'm sorry*.

"Jerome," she whined regretting her honesty.

"Get it together Christine."

Gi grabbed his arm before he could walk away but he quickly pulled away from her. "Don't," she cried watching him turn his back. "Babe," she cried following him out the bathroom and down the stairs. "Listen," she begged running to the front door standing in his way to keep him from leaving. "They're not new feelings and I'll try harder."

"You just told me that you wish our son wasn't born and you want me to stay! Please move Anjel."

Anjel folded her arms ignoring how red in the face he was. "You wanted honest."

Ro looked past her at the sound of his crying son in Alana's arms as she approached the house.

"I'm sorry for my feelings but you can't tell you don't think about our first kid. Mia took a piece of me."

"Find it! Move Anjel! Let La in and let me out."

Gi ignored his demands and stared him down. "You started this."

"Gi," Alana stood at the locked screen door staring at Rome. "Let him leave please."

"It's not fair," she began to cry.

"It sure isn't. Unlock the door. You two need to calm down an' I need to feed Tone." La was patient with her walking into the tail end of the argument she just knew it was serious at the mention of the other child she never knew about. "What you're goin' through is terrible. No one should ever have to lose a child. What is keeping him from leaving gonna solve?"

"We have to fix this," Gi cried staring at very impatient Rome.

"I'm not the fuckin' problem." Ro walked closer to the door and went for the lock and Gi put her body in front of it pissing him off more. "You're bein' childish," he yelled staring at La who also had zero patience and control over the situation. "If you don't," he grabbed Gi's arm and pulled her towards him moving her from the door and she grabbed his arm with her other hand. "You're bein' crazy. I'm tryin', stop." Gi froze as he pinned her against the foyer wall. "Just let me leave," he spoke calmly staring in her glossy eyes. "I don't wanna say something I'll regret."

When he turned his back this time she didn't reach for him. Instead she slid to the floor and sat there finally letting all the tears she was holding back flow.

"I didn't do that. I tried. I'll be back. She's being crazy!" Ro unlocked the door and held it open so La could come in before he went out.

She stood in the foyer holding Tony tightly and staring at his mother in a state of hysterical tears. "Gi," she called reaching out with one hand and Gi sat there trying to stop herself from crying but she couldn't. She placed her knees to her chest feeling her chest get heavy as if her tears were drowning her. "Please breathe." La spoke concerned and slowly taking a seat next to her.

"He's mad an' I can't fix it." She sniffled placing her head on her sister's shoulder.

"What? I'm early. Apparently, I walked in on a hurricane."

Alana sighed holding Tony on her lap and consoling her sister who still insisted on sitting on the floor. As soon as Li walked in Alana stared at her with pleading eyes to take one of her situations.

"Hey, you go finish dinner and take him with. I got this."

Gi sat up and slowly moved away from La not even looking up as her and Tony headed for the kitchen leaving her alone with her other half.

"We could just sit silently or we could talk," Li took a seat next to Anje staring at her staring at the floor. "Whatever it is I'm always in your corner right or wrong." Gi rested her head on Aliyah's shoulder and sat there silently searching for words to describe the epic fuck up she'd just committed.

"I told Ro that I wish our son wasn't born. I never got over the first and I'm afraid I'm gonna screw Tone up."

Li froze internally wincing in pain.

"He left pissed off. I was being honest. I want him I just don't want to be a mom right now."

Aliyah now understood Alana's pleas. *What the fuck do I say to that?* She opted for silence and hugged Anjel.

"I just want to go back to before Tony and Mia. I was happier. I haven't been truly happy since then. Ro said I'm worse than our parents."

"Nothings worse than our parents." Li corrected Ro's insult. "But," she paused hesitant to say what she was thinking. "If one of us has earned the right to lose their shit it's you. Maybe you should talk to someone like a therapist. They're unbiased, can't tell anyone what you say and they offer sound advice."

"But I'm not crazy," Gi whined sitting up.

"You don't have to be crazy to need help and you need help. I wish I could fix this for you but I can't. How 'bout you put on some clothes and we'll talk about it while we help La with this dinner."

"I want him to come home," she pouted.

"He loves you and right now he loves Tone for the both of y'all." Aliyah watched her sister closely as she got up and slowly walked upstairs as if she had the biggest chip on her shoulder.

"What I walk into?" Li quietly questioned Alana as soon as she walked into the kitchen.

"I caught the end. I heard them yelling as soon as I pulled up and she was blocking the front door so he wouldn't leave. I didn't know she lost a baby. Like what?"

"Yeah," Li sighed placing her hand on her hip. "She was kidnapped and pregnant and girl killed her baby instead of her. Since then she's had a baby, panic attacks, oh and before that in the same year she murdered a guy for raping her."

"So she's earned this nervous breakdown?"

"Yeah. I told her to talk to a therapist. I can't fix this one. How 'bout you. What's the dinner for?"

"Just family and this adorable one." Alana smiled seasoning chicken and staring at Tone in his highchair.

"You look comfortable." La greeted Anje first watching her walk into the kitchen in a pair of black leggings and a white crop top.

"I am. I'm gonna see a therapist tomorrow. Let's not talk about Ro."

"What you always wanna talk about Ro. And a therapist for what?"

Gi sighed slightly annoyed as Asia knocked on the back screen door.

"It smells all good in here. What's the occasion?" Asia questioned walking in with an asleep Dallas.

"Pause. Why do you have Dal with you?" Aliyah placed her hand on her hip confused.

"Her father is fuckin' inebriated so I've been watching her 'til he gets his life together."

"Oh! We won't hold our breath on that." Li semi-joked smiling at Dal. "This was a great idea gathering The A Team. We ain't been together since the wedding."

"Let's not mention the wedding." Gi sighed pouring four glasses of wine. "I wanna know what my oldest sister is up to. What's the dinner for?" Gi stared from the fried chicken to the mashed potatoes on the stove.

"I wanted us all together."

Gi sipped on her wine and took a seat at the table.

"Can we talk?" Asia interrupted her few seconds of peace by taking the empty seat across from her.

"If it's about our father I'll pass." Gi smiled watching Li attempt to help La. It almost felt like old times. The three musketeers were together.

"I eat my chicken with ketchup I don't like hot sauce." Asia let it be known.

"Li can you make Tone a bottle please?" La insisted Aliyah stay away from the food.

Gi sat there observing her family watching them make plates for what was sure to be a memorable dinner.

"Gi, Earth to Gi. How many pieces of chicken do you want?"

"Three please," Gi smiled tapping her nails against her empty wine glass. *"I don't. I wish he was never born."* She questioned her emotions and her words from earlier.

"Why she so quiet? She never quiet." Asia questioned the elephant in the room.

"Her and Ro are goin' through something." Li quietly spoke bouncing Tone in her arms.

"They just got married less than two weeks ago."

"I can hear you," Gi quietly spoke refilling her glass and glaring at Asia.

"It's cool. We're gonna all sit down and enjoy this dinner and be a functional family for like five seconds. Here's your plate."

Gi smiled watching La place her plate on the table.

"I'm glad to have you here. I just need for you to not get drunk and work out your issues."

Gi scowled pausing as she refilled her glass. "La," she groaned putting the bottle on the table.

"I'm pregnant."

The room grew silent as Alana let those words nonchalantly slip off her tongue.

"By," Li was the first one to form a coherent thought.

"Nicholas Ramsey." La nodded reading the shocked expression her sisters' faces. "Yes, I'm keeping it. It's a boy. It's not his fault his father is who he is and I was trafficked. I'm not focused on the past. I'm all about my future."

"Congratulations," Asia's smile hid her confusion well. "That kid doesn't stand a chance. He's a Ramsey and a Monroe."

"Yeah, but I can only deal with one circus at a time and I'm opting out of the Ramsey one."

"Do you need anything?" Li was genuinely shocked by her sister's announcement but supported her one hundred percent because that's what Monroe girls did.

"Nope, just family," she assured everyone before going back to her chicken.

"Since we're sharing things," Asia smiled and put down her fork. "I'm thinking of hiring someone to help me look into dad's murder."

"What you wanna know?" La questioned not liking the direction of this conversation but entertaining it for the sake of Asia's feelings.

"Did one of y'all do it?"

The room grew quiet before Anjel, Alana and Aliyah burst into laughter at the table.

"Yes, we didn't like him but I assure you we found him dead on the kitchen floor. I was relieved he was gone but pissed I had to deal with Child and Family services to take these two in."

"This isn't normal. I looked at the police report and the only prints in that whole house were the three of you."

Gi slid her plate away and huffed over this investigation. "If I would've did it I would've wore gloves." She paused folding her hands on the table. "And I probably would've disposed of the weapon to never be found." She rolled her eyes slightly enjoying antagonizing Asia. "Now that I'm ballin' I'd pay the murderer for his or her services."

Alana and Aliyah exchanged glances before cutting the silence with laughter.

"This isn't normal," Asia screamed over them staring at Anje picking her nails directly across from her. "How could you not love either of your parents?"

"No," Gi objected raising her hand staring Asia down. "I loved my mother. She was flawed but she could be sweet."

"I now see why she killed herself... to get away from y'all bitches."

Before La could reach Gi she leaned over the table and smacked Asia across the right cheek. Asia grabbed her arm and pushed her to the floor.

"No, no," Li grabbed Gi so she couldn't walk around the table. "Stop it! Stop!"

"Let her go. Since the day we met we had issues. She's an asshole and that's why it hurts. Me and Dal are leaving anyways. I don't know what this it but it ain't family. I don't wanna speak to her til I get an apology."

Lana stood at the center of the foyer nodding respecting her feelings but knowing that apology was never going to happen.

"Why you invite her any fuckin' ways?" Gi pouted still cornered by her twin who was waiting for Asia's departure.

"Cause she's family." Li folded her arms across her chest and moved closer to Gi keeping her close and cornered in.

"Next time you put your hands on me I will hit you back," Asia rolled her eyes at Anjel before bringing her attention to Alana. "Congrats on the baby. My apologies on the big one in the corner."

"Goodnight Asia." Alana waved trying to contain her amusement. Asia was definitely a Monroe and that was apparent by her attitude on the way out.

"Did you hear her?" Gi yelled as soon as Li moved out the way. "She deserved it! She crossed a line."

"You put your hands on her." Li tried not to take sides not wanting to be in the middle.

"That was after Asia blamed her for Korrine's death. I didn't like Korrine either but those are fighting words most definitely but," Alana paused staring from the both of them. "That if I would've done it talk is dead. There's no statute of limitation on murder. Got it?"

"Okay, I'll stop patronizing her." Gi tried to hold back a smile amused by that speech. "I thought it was funny." Finally, she burst into laughter. Both Alana and Aliyah shook their heads before joining her.

"You are proving to be everything I'd thought you'd be and more. You're my little wildcard." Alana smiled from ear to ear hugging Anjel.

"I'm gonna head out. I gotta see Bellz and then go home. I'm an engaged woman I can't be out all night. Behave and clean up before Ro questions if World War Three went down."

"Got it mom," Gi mocked her twin walking her to the door. "Text me so I know you made it safely."

"Behave. Call me if you need me." Aliyah instructed.

"We won't," Gi assured her closing the door behind her.

"See we don't need Asia. She changes the dynamics of shit. We're the OG Monroes. She was just some bastard."

Alana raised her brow slightly shocked by her comment. *Is there even a good twin anymore?*

...

"Did Bellz come back?" Aliyah walked into the Club Juliet office shocked to only see Marisol.

"No," Marisol looked away from the office computer. "Her dad passed away and Ivy liked him more than she did. Ivy's taking it hard."

"Do you need help with anything?"

Marisol shook her head from side to side. "Your brother-in-law is here throwing bands at strippers but it's his club and his money." Marisol chuckled amused with the situation. "It's a slow night anyways. Go home."

Aliyah sighed knowing that if Ro was here drowning in a bottle so was Aus and both of them had responsibilities beyond finishing off his own bottles. "Thanks, I'm gonna holla at them before heading home. Goodnight." Li waved before heading towards the front of the club.

"Hi, you," she walked on to the floor and quickly spotted Ro throwing money at the strippers on stage with a bottle in one hand. "Hey Aus," she tried Aus who sat next to him with the same lost puppy expression on his face. "Are y'all," she tried Ro again and was quickly interrupted.

"I don't want to talk 'bout your sister." Ro sat his bottle on the table beside him.

"Nope, no Anjel." Aus backed him up sipping on his drink.

"But we good. She's not. But a divorce ain't ever goin' happen so she gotta get wit' the fuckin' program."

"Oh-okay," Li nodded helping herself to a drink. "That's agreed but she just smacked the living shit out of Asia. Dinner was interesting tonight."

"What?" Aus sat up and looked over at her.

"She told Gi that she was the reason Korrine killed herself. To get away from her."

Aus cringed at the thought of Anjel's reaction to such a statement. "Wow!"

"I need you guys to sober the fuck up and find out if Tyler's alive. I need you to talk to your wife and try listening." Li paused staring at Ro who wasn't really paying attention to her. "She's hurting. Grief doesn't just go away and we literally cannot afford for her to lose all her marbles. Between your business ventures and hers we ain't ever gotta be hood rich again."

"Word?" Aus questioned not realizing they were no longer living beyond their means.

"Anjel's a goldmine. A basket-case but a fuckin' goldmine... she's my basket-case." Li semi-joked before taking a sip of her drink.

"Do you want a dance?" Tiny sashayed over to Rome and he shook his head no.

"My wife would kill us all. She owns half the club."

"She does and she will. I'll pay you fifty to go away. Don't bark up that tree." Aliyah smiled watching Tiny walk away. "She want you bad."

Ro sighed sitting back in his chair.

"Your wife could make this whole place disappear especially since she's set to make a fortune this year."

"When you say a fortune and ballin' out of control. How much we talkin' here?" Aus finally asked staring from Ro to Aliyah.

"The two of you are on track to make 1.2 million this year."

"What?" Both Aus and Ro questioned at the same time.

"She might not be mother of the fuckin' year yet but between her store and her modeling career and your two clubs. Your wife is a fuckin' boss when it comes to business. Go home, work this shit out for your kid and sober up because you also have a kid at home." Aliyah brought her attention to Aus and politely smiled before getting up. "I would stay but I'm somebody's fiancée now."

. . .

"You need anything?" La watched Gi put dinner into Tupperware containers.

"Nope, go to sleep. I'm fine. Tomorrow I'll help you get out of the guestroom and into the basement suite. Thanks for having my back."

La smiled leaning against the kitchen doorway. "That's what Monroe girls do. Love you."

Quietly she stood at the kitchen island occasionally staring up at the clock in between rounds of a game on her phone. *Here's a sneak peek: video,* she smiled opening Mickey's email and enlarging the video of her in a bright yellow retro scoop neck one piece bathing suit and sunglasses. Gotti wasn't lying when he said that the studio could take her okay vocals to good vocals.

"Yo!" Ro interrupted walking behind her and paused at the snippet of the video. "One day you goin' design clothes and be dressed right?" He tried to lighten the mood smiling at her in the one piece Angel bathing suit.

"Your wife's a milf," she turned around staring at him slightly terrified and confused to where his head was.

"You goin' make me a plate or what?" He questioned staring in her red eyes.

"I thought we weren't speaking." She was hesitant as he leaned against the island.

"Soo, you just goin' let me starve?" He wrapped his arms around her waist and held her. "I love you," she smiled not caring that he reeked of alcohol. "I don't believe in divorce. Just be a mom an' we good. The only way you can fuck up our son is doin' what you doin' now."

"Okay," quietly she rested her head against his chest just happy he was here. "Can I rent Juliet for Halloween?"

"I'll give you the world just don't raise our kid to be a jerk like his mother."

Her smiled widened amused with his teasing. "I learned that from you."

"Then we're in a lot of trouble our kids gonna be an asshole."

"Jerome," she scoffed playfully hitting him and she squealed louder when he picked her up and plated her behind on top of the counter. *This is what she needed. She missed this.*

...

"Shh! She's sleep."

Austin staggered into his house and was immediately greeted by Asia half-asleep on his couch surrounded by a sea of papers.

"Dinners in the microwave courtesy of the oldest Monroe. I'm gonna head home and shower and go to bed."

"You know you're welcome to stay?" Aus plopped down next to her on the couch. "I heard you had a rough day."

"That's understatement of the year." She groaned staring over at him. "You're grieving I think."

"Nope," Aus stood to his feet and walked into the kitchen returning with two cups and a bottle of tequila. "I'm always venting to you. What's up?"

She sighed before pouring two shots. "I... my sisters aren't who I thought they'd be. They're all jerks; especially Anjel." It all poured out as if she had been waiting for someone to ask. "Anjel smacked me after I accused her of murdering my father."

"Your father is the reason they are the way they are."

Asia shook her head watching him take a shot and pouring them both another round. "No. I lost my daughter. I'm not close to my mom. I wanted family but not like this." She paused gathering her thoughts before taking another shot. "Do you think Anjel is capable of murder?"

"Anje is capable of anything. Definitely not someone you want to piss off." Austin was intentionally vague already knowing the truth. "She deserves everything she has. Her father abused the hell out of her. She found her mother dead an' she lost a child. You still have you mom. They only have each other."

"Are you, are you defending her?" Asia scrunched up her face as she stared him in his eyes.

"No, y'all got more in common than y'all think." He cleaned it up well knowing if it came down to it his loyalty was to Rome and Anjel. "I'm just sayin' you ain't alone. You been here for me. I'm here for you."

"Really?" She smiled happy to have an unbiased ear.

"Really," he assured her. "You ain't gotta fit in with them. You was raised. They just survived. Here.." he went to hand her one more shot and laughed as she placed the glass to his to toast and accidentally spilling a little on his lap.

"No," he objected watching her get up. "It's not a big deal." Before he could finish his thought, she returned with a hand towel and the two of them smiled as she leaned in and wiped at his pants. Their eyes locked and she went to move and he gently pulled her closer for a kiss. Unsure if it was electricity or tequila she gently backed away.

"Aus I don't know if we," Asia paused as all the reasons why this was a bad idea swam around her head but they were drowning in pools of tequila. "What if," she gasped as he gently pulled her on top of his lap. All those bad ideas were just as tipsy because this time when their lips collided nothing could stop the dangerous cocktail they had created on their tongues.

"Ahh," she moaned feeling his lips gently massaging her neck. She hadn't been touched in so long that every time he touched her it felt electric.

"Let's go upstairs," he didn't care if he'd regret it in the morning. Impulsive him was calling all the shots leaving a trail of clothing all the way to the bedroom.

..

Trust me, untie me, He was on top of her again pleading for him to untie her. His smile was etched in her brain like the letters on his tombstone if his body was ever found. Once free she straddled him before placing a pillow over his head.

Opening her eyes, she was elated to be broken out of her nightmare by the sound of Tone's 3AM crying. She'd do anything to end that particular walk down memory lane.

Quietly she got out of bed and slipped on Ro's shirt before tending to Tone across the hall quietly whining. "Why," she groaned picking him up and bouncing him in her arms watching as he quickly grew quiet. "Shhh," she insisted slowly walking downstairs to make him a bottle. *You can do this for your marriage. It's not his fault.* Gently she bit into her bottom lip staring him in his hazel eyes like his father's. *"There's nothing else we can do."* she remembered the doctor's words.

You can do this, she calmed herself. The bouncing was now calming for the both of them. Slowly she bounced him feeling her emotions began to strangle her lungs. Quickly she grabbed the bottle out of the sink and placed it in his mouth. He had so much admiration in his eyes and here she was on the verge of a panic attack.

She felt her body relax as soon as she reached the rocking chair in his room. The two of them sat there for ten minutes rocking back and forth before they were fast asleep.

009. Haunted

Took Dal to my Aunts. The day is yours. You deserve a break.
Lying in bed wrapped in her covers she sighed realizing this was
terrible but it was also an opportunity.

Sure Tyler was possibly dead but she just got dicked down,
Dal adored her, and it wasn't a relationship but it was better than
her last situation. She hadn't hoped to replace Tyler she just did.

Korrine Monroe, Asia tapped the enter key searching the
web again for anything Monroe related and the only thing that came
up was her obituary. **Younger sister to Alyson and Kali King.
Survived by daughters Anjel, Aliyah and Alana Monroe.**

Kali+King+Middlebrooke, Asia sighed sitting back in bed
not expecting much from her search. A smile spread upon her face
at the sight of the first profile picture to come up. "Sheessh, they
really do all look alike." The girls weren't kidding when they said all
they got from Anthony was his golden brown locks and his last
name.

"Let's see what Miss. Kali knows…" she hadn't planned to
spend her day playing detective but she had to get to the bottom of
what happened to her father. Nothing was adding up.

…I just want the truth…

…

"Aliyah!" Anjel smiled walking into Aliyah's house as if the
weight of the world was lifted off her shoulders.

"You're late," Li scolded her staring at her as she entered the kitchen. "Tae is at school and your son is sleeping. Where have you been?"

"I'm sorry I'll pay you back in dinner." Gi smiled pulling shrimp out the freezer. "I went to see a therapist." The words escaped her mouth almost as if they weighed nothing. "I was afraid something was wrong with me because I don't like my son and I wish he was never born."

Li froze shocked with how nonchalant her words were. "And the doctor said?"

Gi shrugged pulling out of box of angel hair noodles. "Something about another session, seeing her more and depression. And journaling my thoughts. Did mom and dad have mental issues?"

"I don't know!" Li stood taken back by her sister's curiosity about the past.

"Were we ever one big happy family?"

Li raised her brow, grabbed two glasses out the cupboard and didn't start talking until tequila filled both the cups. "Never! Mom hated Alana because she didn't listen to anyone. Dad hated everyone I think even himself. Mom didn't leave because her family disowned her when she got with dad. Dad scared her."

Gi tapped her nails against her glass before taking a gulp. "Did he ever get friendly with you too?"

"No! I wasn't girly enough I guess. Lana was too old and grown." Li paused thinking about the hand her sister was dealt.

"You know I told mom once and she yelled at me. She told me to stop talking because people would take us away and that dad loved me."

"So, you want to remember the murder part an' then what? You can't tell your therapist." Li scrunched up her face not understanding the end game to this emotional journey of hers.

"I don't know!" Gi huffed. "I just need clarity and to know why I'm like this."

Aliyah raised her brow so confused. "You look fine to me. Like what?"

"I'm a model! It's my job to look fine. I don't know Li… I'm not happy."

Aliyah's eyes almost bulged out of her sockets watching her identical twin cooking dinner and she looked happy. "How is rehashing every fucked up thing Anthony did to you gonna make you happy? How exactly is peeling that scab gonna help you? I wasn't there when you did it. I wouldn't have let you. The cops told me and La that the murder scene was the most brutal he'd ever seen."

"There were good parts of our childhood."

Li folded her arms across her chest and leaned back in her chair. "Really? Find me one. If it was so great how come you remember none of it?"

"My therapist wants me to write what I do remember. Alana took us out for ice cream once for our birthday and she let us put whatever we wanted on it. We weren't teenagers yet and Alana let us stay out all night!"

Li nodded remembering their tenth birthday a different way. "Lana took us out because dad got arrested the night before for a domestic and public intoxication and our mom was way too high to remember it was our birthday. We stayed out because Alana was afraid to deal with mom without dad."

"Alana took us to the park and taught us how to swim."

"She woke us up bright and early on a Saturday hoping we wouldn't notice dad had beat the shit out of mom the night before."

"What about dad's family? How come we never met them" Gi was now immersed in this conversation as she turned the noodles off and stirred the sauteed shrimp.

"Dad never met his mother. His grandmother raised him. She passed away a little bit after he met mom."

I loved her. She was my world." Gi explained smiling at the thought of her mother.

"You were the only one. Me and Lana hated her."

Gi shook her head from side to side just remembering Korrine's softness. "I remember her and dad would argue and she'd come in my bed and cuddle with me. She could be mean but she needed love and help."

"Mostly help Anjel. She came from a loving family. She was smart as shit and then she met dad. Any loving mother wouldn't have allowed our father to do what he did to us. Dad gave mom drugs, introduced her to a lifestyle and dad cheated on mom a lot. He strangled her. Our mother was weak! I only love her because she gave me you. Because that same bed she cuddled you on she let that bastard touch you in. Me and La could never understand how you could love her."

"She was afraid of him." Anjel argued her side of the story.

Li shook her head disagreeing. "No Gi she was weak. Lana raised us."

Before Anjel could argue her claim the two of them were silenced as soon as Ro, Aus and Darius walked in the kitchen.

"I've been looking for you." Ro entered first picking up her phone off the counter seeing all of his calls she didn't answer.

"We were having some us time." Li spoke up putting her glass down.

"Is there enough for us?" Aus peeked over her shoulder eyeing the shrimp scampi she was putting together.

"What y'all in here gossiping about?" Darius questioned staring at Li knowing it was too quiet when they walked in.

"Halloween," Gi was quick with a lie and it was almost scary. "We're getting it together at Juliet. Sit down and Ro," she groaned feeling him hug her from behind as she attempted to get everyone's plates together.

"Y'all cute." Darius teased watching them kiss.

"Antie Ann!" Gi smiled hearing a squeal from the front door. He bounced all the way from the front door to the kitchen excited to greet Anjel.

"Munchkin!" She returned his excitement.

"Hi to you too child." Li pretended to be offended staring from Darius to Dontae.

"I mean if you want him," Darius chimed in staring at Anjel and Tae hugging as if he was her own.

"Speaking of children," Li giggled hearing her nephew crying in his pack in play in the living room.

"Ro grab him so I can make a bottle. Tae wash your hands so you can eat." Everyone mingled as Gi got dinner together and not one person noticed Li watching her other half the entire night. *She really doesn't like him,* she thought to herself watching Anje spend all of ten minutes with her own son before moving on.

"You put your foot into that scampi. Can you come over and cook more?"

"Is you paying," Ro joked staring from Darius seated across from him to his wife standing at the island in the kitchen just soaking in the now.

"I'll see what I can do," she teased pushing her plate away and picking up her phone noticing a new notification. *Social RealiTea: Gigi Monroe's Estranged Sister: Allegedly caught in The Ramsey Raid.* She immediately clicked on the link hoping it was click bait for once knowing she didn't need this kind of publicity right now. *"Word has it that the eldest Monroe was a prostitute for the oh so famous Ramsey Family and she's prego with one of their kids."*

"Holy fuckin' shit," Gi spoke under her breath scrolling down the page wondering who had this kind of intel and why this was happening to her. As soon as she clicked out of the page her phone lit up with Mickey's name on the screen.

"Hello," she greeted Mickey knowing she was probably calling about the blog.

"Your family," she started sounding exhausted.

"Is a fuckin' circus I know Mick. I know. I'm on my way to the office right now." She tried smiling to avoid explaining the situation to her family. Mickey was good with the press she could smooth over and tame the media circus but there was no spinning this.

New Message: La - Do not mention, confirm, or deny my situation what so ever. Promise?"

Gi huffed staring at her sister's text knowing she didn't want to cross Alana but she also needed to save her career. "Fuck," she tapped her nails trying to think of a million ways to reword these allegations and not include Alana.

Got it, was all she could think to type back before bringing her attention to the rest of her family and trying to think of the easiest escape route that wouldn't end up in an argument with her husband.

...

"So you want a job here?" Robin smiled staring at the ballsy young woman who waltzed right in to Gigi Boutique and asked for a job.

"No, I wanna model," 20-year-old Ryan spoke with excitement as she stood at the counter admiring the posters on the walls of Gigi Boutique.

Robin opened her mouth to speak but all that came out was a light chuckle. "Yeah...no," finally she spoke. "I don't do that kind of hiring. Quite frankly, I'd like to model too." She sighed watching Mickey rush into the front door. "That's the ass you gotta kiss to get that job. Good luck with that."

"Where's Gi?" a frustrated Mickey questioned staring over at the two of them.

"Haven't seen her all day."

"Can you hire me as a model?" Ryan took her shot catching Mickey off guard.

"Do you have any experience?" Mickey sighed staring her down and briefly entertaining her conversation intrigued by her confidence. Ryan could be groomed. Standing at 5'7" she was slender with a creamy deep brown complexion and her almond shaped brown eyes had hunger in them.

"No, but I'm eager and I will start whenever."

"Gigi Boutique sells lingerie." Mickey reminded her what type of modeling she would be getting into.

"And?"

Mickey smiled thinking about the management company that her and Anjel were putting together and this would be a trial of her first potential new client. "Since you have no experience, show up at Juliet for a private Halloween party. It'll be your audition." Mickey huffed staring at the clock on the wall. "Robin get her info. It's gonna be Gi's funeral if she doesn't hurry up. I'll be back in the office if you need me."

Mickey huffed staring at the blog on her phone as she took a seat at the office desk impatiently waiting for Anjel's arrival. Gigi Monroe was a fuckin' gold mine but Anjel Monroe had a mine of secrets and it seemed like every five seconds someone was digging up skeletons.

"I know! I know you need a raise." Gi rushed in the back door surprisingly relaxed.

"I also need a statement." Mickey informed her pushing her phone over to her as Gi took the empty seat on the other side of the desk. "It's only a matter of time before Karen at B Magazine starts asking questions."

Gi nodded gently biting into her bottom lip. "I talked with my sister and we agreed to not include her in any of this."

Mickey raised her brow confused. "She's the fuckin' topic."

"No, I'm the topic. Look La raised me. What she says goes and she wants zero parts of this. I don't even know who got the story. But here's what we're going to say. Gigi Monroe and Angel Entertainment feels for the families affected by sex trafficking as it's a problem around the world. We do not condone the actions of The Ramsey Family and reach out to the community to donate to those affected by sex trafficking. Something of that nature sounds good."

Mickey sighed sitting back in her chair not liking the vagueness of the statement but giving her client what she wanted. Before she could even comment on the backlash that might come from the statement Gi pulled out a stack of papers and placed them on the desk. "What are these?" Mickey leaned in noticing her name on the pages.

"We're building slash built quite the fuckin' empire. I needed it in writing. Everything we make we split in thirds."

Mickey shook her head from side to side staring at Gi as if she had lost her mind. "I didn't ask for that much."

"You deserve it," Gi argued expecting a million thank yous.

"Legally. You gotta run things like this past your silent partner. Even in thirds that's a lot of fuckin' money. How was therapy?"

"Therapy was amazing. I love paying a stranger to help me sort out the tragedy I call life."

"I need to know about these things before they occur." Mickey scratched her hair trying to tread delicately on the many skeletons in the Monroe Closet.

"If I had a heads up don't you think I would tell you? How do I know when people are gonna go digging?"

"Anything else that might come up?" Mickey was pleading at this point.

"I don't know. My lifestyle is crazy. Don't worry about it. I'll run this contract past Rome and we're gonna get this Halloween party together and every things gonna go back to normal."

Mickey blankly stared at her in confusion to how she could be so calm at time of crisis. This wasn't only her career at stake it was also Mickeys. "Your career is connected to mine. We're a team and teams don't leave each other in the dark. What do I not know?"

"Everything is just fine. Let's focus on this party. We don't go digging in Gotti's past."

"Uhh yeah they do. Gotti had slash has gang affiliations. It didn't take a rocket scientist to figure that out. What am I missing? I'm not gonna run away if it's something big. I'm already invested in this."

Gi tapped her fingernails on the desk before looking up at Mickey. "It's fine," she spoke softly. "I just had shitty childhood okay. That's why I need therapy. My father used to rape me and I found my mother dead from a drug overdose. My sisters are all I have. I don't want my story out there especially since I'm still unraveling it."

It was bittersweet for Mickey to hear but she was content to finally get an answer to the puzzle that was Anjel

. . .

"Someone should seriously fuckin' clean," Tori quietly groaned letting herself in Austin's apartment with Tyler's spare key and a plastic pumpkin filled with candy in hand. "Hello, " she smiled following the giggling down the hall assuming it was Aus and Dallas. "Hey I," the orange pumpkin fell to the floor at the sight of Asia and Austin completely naked in bed. "You gotta be fuckin' kidding me. Do you even care? She could be dead."

"Tori," he sighed covering the two of them with the gray comforter. "Listen," he tried to explain himself knowing Tori was devastated.

"An you," Tori brought her attention to Asia staring at Tori in awe that she had a key to the apartment. "You're always talking 'bout how you're better than Gi and Li and Lana. You're just like them. Don't show up at Juliet tonight. Where's Dal?"

"At my Aunts. They goin' trick or treating." Aus sighed not knowing how to fix the situation.

"You already found your trick no sense in lookin' for Tyler. Member' her? She deserves so much fuckin' better than this nonsense. If she's somewhere in ditch dead I'll never forgive you because instead of lookin' for her you were either drunk or fuckin' this bitch."

"I'm not gonna be too many more bitches," Asia spat offended by Asia's words.

"Bye Aus. I'll come by to see my god daughter tomorrow. Good luck with whatever this shit is. You let her prance around her we don't even know her."

"Bye! Victoria," Asia tried the polite route feeling vulnerable naked.

"I hope you choke on his cum," Tori screamed turning around walking towards the front of the apartment.

Sitting her makeshift home office, she sat in bed with a glass of wine in her hand staring at her unopened masquerade costume. She wasn't even imaging the havoc at Juliet hoping the out of sight out of mind theory would work. Silence filled the entire house and she just wanted to bask in the stillness of it all. "Why," she whined staring down at Mickey's name flashing on her phone screen.

"Where are you," an irritated Mickey greeted her with havoc in the background.

"I don't want," Gi started and Mickey quickly interrupted her moment.

"Anjel, I'm pulling the manager card." She was in manager mode not up for her excuses.

"I don't feel well," Anje groaned into the phone like a child.

"Are you dying?" Mickey rolled her eyes over the theatrics.

"Mentally, yes."

"Gi," Mickey interrupted and Gi abruptly pushed the end button on her phone and pushed it off her desk shattering the screen and ending the call. She quickly powered down her personal phone and covered her face with her hands silently sitting in her bedroom afraid to tend to her physical tangible.

Slowly she walked toward the en-suite bathroom and stood frozen at the multiple tests on the counter reading the same thing. "Fuck me," she thought of it as the cherry on top of her shitty sundae.

"Aye! What up Mick? My wife with you?"

Mick smiled at Rome. "Nope! She says she doesn't feel well."

"She the host. What's up?" He saw past her fake smile.

"Hey Gotti can we talk?" She quickly spotted Gotti and saw him as an out to the conversation at hand.

"What the fuck is up with Gi no?" Ro thought out loud.

"What is you talkin' 'bout? I thought y'all was good." Tori questioned not knowing it was a rhetorical question.

"Where's Gi?" La interrupted.

Ro shrugged. "She don't feel good. She ain't comin' or answering her phone."

"She been all over the place lately." La huffed annoyed with her inability to read her twin.

"Ever since Mia she's been off. But she'll show up." Aliyah tried to give him hope.

"Shits unprofessional." Tori huffed.

"It is half her club though." Aliyah argued smiling as Aus and Asia made their way over.

"I thought I told you two to stay home." Tori screamed over the loud music staring the two of them down in disgust.

"This ain't even start yet and shits a disaster." Bellz huffed agitated that the co-host wasn't there and Tori was on eleven.

...

"So what's the fuckin' plan?"

Rayna smiled staring at her younger sister with a very much alive and eerily calm Tyler sitting in the corner. "I want everything I'm owed and she's gonna get it for me. We goin' have a little fun tonight an' I might have to put her out of her fuckin' misery." Ray sat in the office chair at Karma watching Aus and Asia dancing on the dance floor as the crystal clear footage caught everything. "It ain't take him long to move the hell on. He always been an idiot."

She stared from camera to camera and stopped at a pregnant Alana. "Whoa! It's definitely a party now." Ray turned off all the cameras and chuckled at the many scenarios running through her head staring down at the neatly organized desk and froze at the contract between Anjel, Mickey, and a third party company.

"This the bitch that hired you? How much you gettin' paid?"

"Nothin' it's an audition and yes she the gatekeeper to all things Gigi Monroe."

"Where's Gigi?"

"I don't know probably late as usual."

Ray nodded excited to finally get pay back. "Watch her. I'm gonna go handle something." She didn't wait for a response before leaving Tyler with her little sister.

...

"So, she cool?"

Mickey stared at Gotti and nodded. "She'll be fine. It's probably food poisoning." She sighed lying knowing damn well that Anjel was Anjel's biggest ailment. "I'll give her your regards. Til' then drink and be merry."

Gotti smiled okay with the last minute cancellation realizing he wouldn't have to share the spotlight as masked club goes poured into Karma.

"You leaving so soon?" Ro started toward the back exit and was stopped by Tiny dressed in the most clothes he'd ever seen her in which said a lot because her slutty nurse left nothing to the imagination. "Where's your costume?"

"Nice seein' you Tiny. I'm 'bout to go check om my wife. She's..."

"Clinically bipolar? I just knew y'all would get through that."

Ro stopped finally all ears as she approached him.

"You didn't know?" Tiny scoffed seeing the confusion on his face. "Apologies. Gi and Bellz were talkin' about your wife's been in therapy and everything. Li Gi been wild lately."

Ro stood staring her down as she stood in front of him with no reason to lie. "Let's talk about this." He insisted pulling her towards the back office and grabbing a bottle of tequila on his way. "What else you know?"

"This was fun I guess... I'll stay a while." La was ready to go but quickly changed her tone when she exchanged glances with Li who also spotted a red faced Rome dragging Tiny towards the back office.
"Are they fighting?"

"No! Not that I know of." Li sighed not up for an episode

of The Anjel Show.

"Watch them two I'm gonna go pee this costume is the fuckin' worst. We gotta see what all that is about. Try call Anje again. I'll be back." Alana shook her head in disbelief at the drama unfolding. It was crazy how times may have changed but Alana was still putting out fires as that's what big sisters did.

"Get off!"

Alana's eyes almost budged out of their sockets as she walked into the bathroom and immediately spotted Mickey choking Rayna from behind.

"I obviously taught you nothin'. This is dumb and unexpected." Alana smiled watching Rayna scratching Mickey's arms trying to find her weakness.

"Bitch!" Mickey screamed feeling Rayna elbow her in the stomach.

Alana stood conflicted knowing Mick wouldn't hold up long and how she had a baby to think about now.

"Mick, go!" La shrugged finally making her choice. "This ain't your fight. I really liked you Ray." She groaned rushing Ray and pushing her into the wall realizing she hadn't had an opportunity to unleash her anger since re-entering the family.

"I'm gonna enjoy watching you suffer so bitch you better kill me."Rayna chuckled as Alana went to punch her and she quickly blocked it and grabbed her arm. "Every fuckin' thing you put me through. I don't even want a sorry 'cause they worth shit to me."

Alana gasped grabbing Rayna's hand as she tugged harder at her hair.

Ray smiled pushing La into the mirror causing pieces to shatter all over the bathroom.

"I know you're not just gonna give up." Ray stared at breathless Alana in awe at the blood on her hands. "One of us can't leave this bathroom." Ray locked the door from the inside before slowly approaching Alana. "Your family..."

Alana quickly interrupted her rushing her into the wall fighting her exhaustion and letting her frustrations surface. She saw nothing but red thinking about the last few years of her life. She pushed Rayna's hands away and she went to choke her and forcefully kneed her in the stomach causing her to gasp. Quickly she took the upper hand and grasped her hair as Rayna had once done and rammed it into the granite counter watching her body go limp she didn't care one bit if she was dead or not. She had to check on Aliyah.

...

"Your wife really is a fuckin' basket case. Sitting around here I get all the details. I don't wanna be on her shit list but yeah... she..."

"Not gossip." Jerome tried to wrap his head around her words.

"It's not gossip if Li an' Bellz are sayin' it. Shit even Mickey knows somethin' is up. She wouldn't have had Tone if she had a choice even if that meant no you. I don't see the fuckin' issue. Who wouldn't want you?" Tiny flashed her pearly whit teeth as she sat on the desk sipping on tequila straight as if was a good idea. "You find you deserve someone who'll let you lead and got a good head on their shoulders. She smiled at him standing in front of her slightly intoxicated by the alcohol and the opportunity she was throwing at him. "Wanna know another secret?" She motioned for him to come closer and smiled as she leaned in and stood in between her legs. "you could do so much fuckin' better like," she paused kissing his neck and scooting closer to the edge of the desk basically begging for it.

Staring down at her half naked he smiled. There was no way he would consider a relationship with someone so thirsty but he knew taking even the slightest sip would piss his wife off so when Tiny pulled him in for a kiss he fuckin' drank her all in. "Fuck," he found himself in between her thighs with no pants on and fuckin' his frustrations with his stranger who had no strings or secrets to keep from him.

"Shit!" He grunted feeling her insides suffocating him. She grasped him tighter pushing herself closer so she could feel more of him. She had wanted this for so longer and it was everything she dreamed of. Her bliss was cut short when the office door opened and Ailiyah walked in red in the face and phone in hand.

"You're fuckin' kiddin' me!"

"Aliyah," Bellz quickly pulled Li out of the room and went to grab the phone but Li pulled away. "What did you just do?" She screamed watching her press send. "Who did you...no! No! You're kiddin'. We gotta go like now!" Bellz was disappointed in her best friends today. "What was that gonna solve?"

...

Staring at the photo Anjel sat in the empty bathtub glass of wine in hand wrapping her head around everything all at once. She felt herself drowning in all her problems. Everything seemed perfect to everyone else but herself. She titled her head to the side zooming in on the photo of her husband fuckin' one of his strippers and smiled trying to find humor in a situation that would never be humorous.

She put the phone down, finished her wine and turned the water on mesmerized as it filled the tub surrounding her and blanketing her with warmth. She thought of her son fast asleep across the hall and how everything would be better without her. If she could just stop the world for a moment... Just a moment she could fill something other than the nothingness that pumped through her veins. She turned the water off fixated on something sharp something to pause everything even if it meant it was the end.

Ever since I lived when I wasn't supposed to, I've felt

numb. Like I deserved none of it. Like a magnet my eyes were fixated on the blades of my razors. I lay my head back in the tub contemplating where everything went wrong.

Why was I still alive yet so dead at the same time? Was the universe torturing me for entertainment?

I picked the blade out as if I had done it before and stared fixated on it before slowly drawing it down my wrist. My eyes were fixated on the blood mixing with the water. My mouth dropped in awe that it hurt but it felt good as I hadn't felt shit since Mia tried to kill me. The pain was bliss in some twisted way. I sat back taking it all in finally getting that pause I so greatly needed. The warm water and warm blood was everything I needed to be. I felt myself slowly letting the pain take over me and I wasn't the one in control anymore. *Maybe I needed this. This was how it was supposed to be.*

... 911 what's your emergency?

Check out "Stripped" by Devin J

If you loved this book, don't forget to leave a review on Amazon. If you didn't love this book, also please leave a review. I appreciate any criticism.

xoxo,

Devin J.

www.facebook.com/booksbydev
https://twitter.com/booksbydev
www.instagram.com/booksbydev
Booksbydev@gmail.com